Future V

B

The Final Chapter

Russell Fine

Dedication

I want to take this opportunity to thank all of my proofreaders and editors for the assistance they provided in creating this book. This book is dedicated to them.

First, my wife Sherry spent countless hours editing, correcting silly mistakes, and helping me with the plot.

My son, Randy, read the book several times looking for errors and checking the plot as well.

My friend and neighbor, Suzanne Horsfall, provided assistance by proofreading.

Another friend and neighbor, Cheryl Adamkiewicz, who spent many hours checking both the words and content for errors.

Finally, friend and fellow author, B J Gillum, who gave me very valuable assistance by providing the final proofreading.

Preface

This is the third, and final, book in the Future World History series. Book One covered slightly more than one hundred years, beginning in 2019. During that time, the power module was invented. It replaced all forms of energy that were previously in use. As a result of that invention the population of Earth experienced substantial economic, political, medical, and scientific changes. Earth began sending expeditions to other solar systems, met with other humanoid species, and became the four hundred eighth member of an interstellar trade group.

Book Two covered only a period of fifteen years. During this period of time Earth became the richest planet in the trade group, a position we still enjoy today. This was, for the most part, due to the efforts of Jeffery and Debbie Whitestone, the Captain and first officer of Earth's first starship. The amazing discoveries they made paved the way for Earth's success.

It started with the exploration of the Procolt System, and specifically the second planet in the system, Procolt 2. The planet was similar to Earth in terms of atmosphere, gravity, and temperature. It contained a variety of native life forms. Shortly after beginning the exploration of Procolt 2, two amazing discoveries were made. The first was the remains of a solider from the United States found in a cave. The second, and more important, was the discovery of an intelligent non-humanoid life form. They resembled squirrels from Earth but they were much larger, had hands with opposable thumbs, and an ability to learn that exceeded any other living creature in the galaxy.

There were two major problems shared by all the trade group members at that time. Even though they were able to travel through space at up to five hundred times the speed of the light, the vast distances between solar systems required a minimum of thirty days to travel to the closest neighbor. For more distant systems the travel time could easily exceed one hundred days.

Additionally, it was impossible to communicate effectively between the member planets because the communication system they used didn't allow messages to travel faster than the speed of light.

Both of these problems were resolved by the squirrels from Procolt 2 working in conjunction with the Chief Engineer from NASA. Their three-year collaboration resulted in both ships and messaging systems that could move ten thousand times faster than light.

During this period, the people of Earth managed to incur the wrath of the Planet Crosus. Crosus attacked Earth, but even though they were defeated, more than ten thousand people on Earth lost their lives.

Jeffery and Debbie decided to retire and build a resort on Procolt 2. Procolt Paradise was a spectacular success. However, Crosus was not about to give up. They wanted revenge so they sent a terrorist couple to the resort. The terrorists set off an explosion that destroyed the resort's marina. They sent Jeffery a series of demands and said they would kill thousands of people at the resort if their demands were not met. However, S1, the leader of the Procolt 2 squirrels, told Jeffery he had a plan to resolve the problem.

That is where Book Two ended and this book begins.

Most of this book takes place in locations other than Earth. For reference purposes, you should know that one *Unit* equals 1.23 miles. A galactic standard day has 20 hours which is equal to 28.5 Earth hours. Also, for time measurement, the galactic standard uses hours and hundredths of an hour instead of hours and minutes.

Russell Fine
September, 3506

Procolt Paradise

Jeffery looked at S1 and asked, "What's your plan to defuse this situation?"

"I was hesitant to tell you this earlier, but now I have no choice. Apparently, we are still being affected by the radiation. About a half year ago we began to notice that when we're near humanoids we were able to read their emotions. Please understand, we can't read minds. I can't tell what they are thinking, but I can tell if they are, for example, happy, sad, excited, worried, or confused. I was concerned because I wasn't sure if you would be comfortable knowing we could do that."

"Wow! That's definitely an interesting development, but I don't see how it helps us."

"In the tower for the guests from Coplent everyone is sad, worried, or excited. Only one couple is happy. They are in room 5217."

Suddenly Jeffery remembered the message he received from S34 regarding Robelt and Melda Flemm. "Are the people staying in that room named Flemm?"

"Yes, how did you know?"

"I received a report from S34 about them that said they were probably from Crosus, but I decided to ignore it. Obviously, that was a serious mistake. They said they've placed explosives in both guest towers. I don't think they're going to just let us in without blowing up the other tower."

S1 smiled and said, "I haven't told you everything yet. We also discovered we can activate something in a humanoid brain that causes them to fall asleep instantly. Would you like me to demonstrate it for you?"

"Uh, no, I don't think so. I assume you have tried this on people."

"Yes, we have, but only when people are relaxing around the pool. They only sleep for a few minutes and there doesn't appear to be any harmful effects that resulted from our experiments."

"In this case I'm not very concerned about harmful effects. Do you have to be close to them to make this work?"

"No, I'm sure I can do it from here. But I can only do one person at a time. If you want me to do this I'll go and get S4 to help."

"Okay, go get S4. While you're doing that I'll get one of our doctors to whip up something that will keep them unconscious until we can get help here."

Jeffery left his apartment and walked over to the medical office. He was surprised to find both of the resort's doctors, Frank and Marcet, there. He spent a minute or two filling them in on what happened and then he asked, "Do you guys have something that will keep the Flemms unconscious for a few days?"

Marcet replied, "They are from Crosus, not Coplent, so their physiology is different, but I'm sure I can make something you can use that will keep them out for at least a day."

"That should be okay. I think once they are unconscious we can bind them with wire ties and take them to a cave a few hundred units from here. When help arrives, we can go pick them up and take them to Earth or Coplent for trial."

Marcet said, "Give me a half hour to make my magic potion. I'll bring it to you when it's ready."

"Thanks, I'll be waiting for you," Jeffery said as he left the office.

When Jeffery arrived at the apartment he was surprised to see the door was open. Inside S1 and S4 were talking to Debbie. When S1 saw him he said, "We're ready. We've never tried this on anybody from Crosus before, but I see no reason why it won't work."

4

"I want to wait until Marcet has her sleeping potion ready."

Marcet and Frank arrived at the apartment a half hour later. Marcet gave Jeffery two vials of medication and an air pressure syringe. "This should keep them out for at least a day. They will probably feel like shit when they wake up, but I don't think you really care about that."

"Personally, I think that's a real plus," Jeffery said. Turning to Debbie he said, "I'll call you after they're sedated. Send a message to Earth and tell them what happened and ask them to send help."

"Okay."

Jeffery walked over to his computer and opened a screen that showed the rooms on the fifty-second floor of the Coplent Guest Tower. There were two vacant rooms on that floor. He called his chief maintenance engineer, Jim Roberts. When Jim answered Jeffery spent a few minutes telling him what happened and then Jeffery said, "I need your two strongest guys in my apartment as soon as possible and tell them to bring some big wire ties that are suitable for binding hands and feet."

"Is this going to be dangerous?"

"I don't think so, but feel free to ask for volunteers."

"Okay, I'll have two guys there in a few minutes."

"Thanks Jim," Jeffery said as he terminated the call.

A few minutes later two men showed up at Jeffery's apartment. The door was still open so they walked in. Jeffery told them what was going on and asked them to go to room 5224 in the Coplent Tower. He also told them to use the service elevator so they wouldn't have to walk by room 5217. Jeffery and the two squirrels left a few minutes later.

As soon as they arrived at the room Jeffery told S1 to put the Flemms to sleep. Jeffery watched as both S1 and S4 closed their eyes and began to concentrate on the task. A few seconds later

S1 open his eyes and said, "We are finished. Both of them are sleeping."

Jeffery and the two maintenance men walked over to room 5217 and opened the door with a pass key. Once inside they found both of them sound asleep on the couch. Jeffery gave each of them a dose of Marcet's sleeping potion and asked, "Can you guys carry them out?"

"Yeah, that's not a problem," one of the men answered.

"Okay, use the wire ties to bind their hands and feet, take them to the shuttle, and strap them in. I'll be there in a few minutes. The medication I gave them will keep them out for at least a day."

Jeffery called Debbie and told her the Flemms were no longer a threat and asked her to send the message to Earth.

"I don't think we should do that yet. I think we need to make sure they don't have some kind of automatic device that will trigger the explosives if we send a message. I'm going to get Brealak and the two of us will search their room first."

"I didn't think of that. Please contact me and let me know what you find."

"Okay."

Jeffery decided he didn't want his prisoners to die waiting for the ship from Earth, so he stopped at the break room and picked up fifteen bottles of water and twenty protein bars. When Jeffery arrived at the shuttle the two maintenance men were just finishing strapping their prisoners to their seats. When everyone was ready Jeffery flew a thousand units north of the resort and landed near a cave he had explored two years ago. He turned to his maintenance men and asked, "Did you search them for weapons or electronic devices?"

"Yeah, but we didn't find anything," one of them answered.

"Okay, let's put them at least a hundred feet inside the cave. That way if we missed something they won't be able to use it anyway."

Since the Flemms were still unconscious, they had to be carried inside the cave. Jeffery brought a lamp and left it with them so when they woke up they would know they were inside a cave and realize they had been captured. He unbound their hands but not their feet and left the water and protein bars next to the lamp.

When they returned to Procolt Paradise Jeffery called Debbie. "Hi, we're back. I left our guests in a cave a thousand units north of here. I'm sure they will be very uncomfortable when they wake up."

"Good, they deserve it. Brealak and I searched their room. We found some communication devices and two other devices that looked like they could be used to trigger their explosives remotely. We took everything and put it inside the hotel safe."

"Okay. When you send a message to Earth about our situation ask them if they have something we could use to help us locate the explosives. I'm not going to feel safe until they have been located and disarmed."

"I'll send the message out immediately. I'll also send a memo this morning to all our guests explaining what happened."

"That's a good idea, but I'm not sure what to do about our guests. What if the explosives have timers on them that are already armed?"

"I'll mention that possibility in my message to Earth. I'm sure that even if they put timers on the devices they wouldn't go off for several more days. Obviously, if they went off before you had time to meet their demands, they wouldn't get what they want."

"That's a good point."

Debbie sent the message to Earth a few minutes later. They would get the message in two days. Now all they could do was wait.

Four days later they received a response from Earth. They were going to send out an armed ship immediately. The ship had a six person crew and was equipped with explosive detection equipment. They would take control of the prisoners and help locate the explosives before returning to Earth.

The ship arrived two days later. It was a small ship, but like all the ships currently being built, it had the newest propulsion system that enables it to travel at ten thousand times the speed of light, so it could travel the twenty-seven light years from Earth in three days. The Captain of the ship was Glen Turner. Captain Turner, like everyone else at NASA, knew about Jeffery and Debbie, and he was anxious to meet them.

Jeffery was informed the ship was landing and he and Debbie went to the landing pad to meet them. Captain Turner was the first one off the ship. He looked at Jeffery and Debbie, smiled, and said, "Admiral Whitestone, it's a pleasure to meet you and Captain Whitestone. I have heard a lot about both of you. You are legends back at NASA headquarters. I'm Captain Turner, but please call me Glen. This is Lieutenant Durst, my first officer."

"It's nice to meet you as well. I'm sure you're aware of our situation. After we determine if there are any explosives on the resort grounds and disarm any we find, I will be happy to treat you and your crew to an all-expense paid vacation."

"Thank you, sir, we'll get right on it. It would be helpful if there was somebody we could work with who is very familiar with the structures here."

"I will have our chief engineer, Jim Roberts, here in a few minutes to help you. We also have two prisoners stashed in a cave a thousand units from here. You'll have to retrieve them and take them back to Earth for trial."

"Take your time, they aren't going anywhere anyway."

"I'll contact you as soon as we're finished."

"Thank you," Jeffery responded. Then he called Jim Roberts and told him there was a crew here to scan the resort for explosives and they wanted his help with the building layout. Jim said he would be there in a few minutes.

Jeffery and Debbie went back inside. They went to the staff break area where each had a cup of coffee. Shortly after they sat down S1 walked in. He sat across from Jeffery and asked, "Is that the ship from Earth that just landed?"

"Yeah, they will be scanning for explosives shortly. It's too bad you couldn't read the minds of our prisoners. Then we would know if they planted any bombs."

"Perhaps we will develop that ability in the future."

"What you did was amazing. You may have saved thousands of lives. I have no words to express how much we appreciate it."

"We will always help you in any way we can. If you and Debbie had not come to Procolt 2 we would still be living in caves."

"Okay, I guess we've helped each other."

Then S1 asked, "What are the plans for rebuilding the marina?"

"I don't know yet. I sent a message to our architect, Nandor, yesterday telling him what happened. I expect to receive a reply in two or three days. I hope we can start on the replacement very quickly."

"When you do could you also build an area for us? We would like to have four or five rooms like we have in Squirrel Haven."

"That won't be a problem. I'll let Nandor know."

"By the way, we now have three pregnant females."

9

"That's wonderful! It'll bring your population to one hundred twenty-two."

"Yes, our group is certainly growing. It will be years before we outgrow Squirrel Haven, but several members of our group asked if they could have a place to stay close to the lake."

"When I receive plans on the new marina from Nandor I'll let you review them."

"Thank you."

"You're welcome."

S1 left the break room and for a while Debbie and Jeffery were alone. Then Jeffery's com unit beeped. When he answered Glen Turner said, "Hi Jeffery. So far we have found three explosive devices. There was one in each guest tower in the elevator equipment room. We also found one in the main dining room kitchen. They all look like they have remote triggers, but we will disassemble them and let you know what we find."

"Thank you, Glen. You should also check around the marina, or what's left of it, to see if any devices are there as well."

"No problem, but we want to leave in a half hour to pick up your prisoners. We don't know where the cave is so we will need your help."

"Okay, just let me know when you're ready to go."

"I'll call you."

A half hour later Glen, Jeffery, and two other members of Glen's crew were on their way to pick up the Flemms. Glen landed the ship near the cave. As they entered Glen and his men took out their weapons. When they arrived at the area where the Flemms were left five days earlier they found them sitting on the floor with their backs against the wall. They managed to free their feet but made no move to get up as the four men approached them.

Robelt Flemm said, "Is there any additional cost for the cave tour? You should know that Melda and I really didn't like it very much. The accommodations are awful."

10

Glen said, "I'm placing both of you under arrest for destruction of property and acts of terrorism. You will be taken back to Earth for trial."

Robelt started to say something but changed his mind.

Jeffery said, "We found the explosive devices you planted and they have all been disarmed."

"Are you sure you found all of them?" Robelt asked as he smiled.

Jeffery ignored the question.

Each of the crewmen escorted a prisoner to the ship. Once they were inside each prisoner was placed in a seat and belted in. Glen looked at the prisoners and said, "Those belts are locked so don't bother trying to get up."

The trip back to Procolt Paradise was uneventful. However, after Glenn and Jeffery got off the ship Glen said, "I don't want to deal with our prisoners during the return to Earth. Can you give me more of the sedative you used on them?"

"Sure, I'll ask Marcet to give you some. Is there anything else you need?"

"No, I'm going to leave two of my guys here with all the equipment. I'll have them check the buildings again. I want to leave as soon as I get the medicine. I should be back in six or seven days."

"Okay, let's go to the Medical Office and see Marcet."

When Jeffery and Glen got to the office Marcet was there bandaging one of the guests who had fallen by the pool. She looked up and said, "Hi Jeffery, I'll be done here in a minute."

Marcet finished bandaging her patient and said, "That should be healed by tomorrow morning. Please be more careful around the pool. It does get slippery sometimes."

"Yeah, I noticed that a bit late. Thank you, doctor."

"You're welcome. Please let me know if there's a problem."

11

"I will," the patient said as she got up and left the office.

"Okay Jeffery, how can I help you?" Marcet asked.

"Glen would like more of the sedative so his prisoners won't be a problem during the trip to Earth."

"I think I still have ten doses." She walked over to a cabinet and took out some vials and a pressure syringe and gave them to Glen. "Each dose should render them unconscious for at least fifteen hours, so this should be enough to get you back to Earth."

"Thank you." Glen said.

"You're welcome."

Jeffery said, "I arranged for rooms for your two crewmen who are staying. Just have them stop at the registration desk. When you come back if you would like to stay for a while just let me know."

"Thank you, that's very generous. Is it okay if I come back with my wife?"

"Sure. I really appreciate your help with this situation."

"It's all part of our job. I'll see you again soon," Glen said as he walked back to his ship.

Thirty days after the Flemms were brought to Earth they were tried for the crimes they committed at Procolt Paradise. The evidence was overwhelming and the trial only lasted for two days. The jury found them guilty on all counts and they were sentenced to twenty years in prison.

Crosus

Bejort Griss, the current leader of Crosus, was mad. Every attempt to retaliate against Earth and Coplent had failed. He was sure the attack on Procolt Paradise would succeed. The attack was meticulously planned. He was positive every potential problem with the plan had been resolved. Obviously, he was wrong. The next time there would be no mistakes. His plan was to destroy the entire Procolt System, and he was sure he would soon have the ability to do it.

Hasin Tork, the person in charge of weapons development, was already a few minutes late for his appointment. Bejort didn't like waiting; he was not a patient man. He considered tardiness an act of disrespect. He thought about throwing Hasin in jail for a week as a warning not to be late again, but he needed the weapon Hasin was working on.

Hasin arrived .2 hours after the scheduled time. Bejort was almost wild with rage, but he contained himself. When Hasin entered Bejort's office he said meekly, "Sir, I'm sorry I'm late for our appointment. Please forgive me. I was waiting for the latest test results and it took a little longer than I expected."

"If you are ever late for an appointment again you will be punished. Is that clear?" Bejort said angrily.

"Yes sir. I promise it won't happen again."

"So, what were the results you wanted to have before our meeting?"

"Small scale tests indicate the device will be capable of destroying an entire solar system. However, the process will take much longer than we anticipated. It could take up to a year, far longer than our original estimate of thirty days."

Bejort looked at Hasin. The hate he felt for Hasin was obvious when he screamed, "That is entirely unacceptable! You assured me the weapon would work within thirty days. Now I will give you thirty days to make whatever modifications are necessary to meet your original estimate. Failure to meet that goal will result in a most unpleasant experience for you and your entire family. Now get out of here."

Hasin did not reply to Bejort's outburst. He simply turned around and left the office. As Hasin walked back to his office he made a decision. He was going to leave Crosus. He didn't know where he was going to go yet, but the first step was to leave the planet. By the time he arrived at his lab he knew exactly what he was going to do.

He spent two weeks making some modifications to the design of the weapon. Computer simulations indicated that the changes would speed up the process by more than a hundred days, but that was still far slower than his original estimate. Since he couldn't find a way to speed up the process, he decided his only reasonable course of action was to cheat.

He spent the next few days modifying the simulator that was used to test the weapon. When he was finished he ran the same test he had run previously. Now the results indicated total destruction of all planets within a two hundred million unit orbit around the star in twenty-seven days. He was pleased with the results and hoped Bejort would be as well.

He wrote up a report based on his latest test results and sent it to Bejort along with a request to test the weapon on a nearby system that had only one planet within its effective range. Since the Lundalt System was uninhabited, nobody would know or care if the system was destroyed. The prototype of the weapon would take one hundred fifty days to build.

Bejort was pleased with the report he received from Hasin and ordered him to proceed with the test. Hasin and his team began building the prototype. When it was about half finished Hasin told his wife what was going on and told her to go to Beljang with their two children to visit her sister. Beljang was not part of the trade group so there were no restrictions on traveling there. It was also one of the few trading partners that Crosus still had.

Hasin was worried that Bejort might try to stop his wife and children from leaving the planet, but there was no problem. Hasin and his team finished the prototype several days ahead of schedule. Hasin arranged for a small ship to use that would take him and the weapon to the Lundalt System where it would be tested. The day before he was scheduled to leave he destroyed all the design data for the weapon.

When he left Crosus he programmed the navigation system to take him to the system where the test was supposed to occur. The ship stopped seventy-five million units from the systems sun. He sent a partial message back to Crosus indicating the navigation system had failed and brought him only twenty million units from the systems sun. Then he disabled all the telemetry systems that sent automatic messages back to Crosus. The weapon was already loaded into a small probe that was supposed to be launched at the sun. However, he aimed it at the system's only planet, a large ball of methane and ammonia, and launched it. He thought now Crosus would never be able to recover the weapon or build another one. He was only half right.

He programmed the ship to take him to Beljang. He had originally decided to destroy the ship when he got there, but changed his mind. He decided to sell the ship and use the money to take him and his family to some other planet in the trade group where he felt they would be safe. He knew that since Crosus did not have the new communication system, he would arrive and leave Beljang before Crosus received his message.

Beljang

Two days after he arrived on Beljang he sold the ship for twelve hirodim blocks. More than enough for him and his family to get to another planet and live there for a while. He discussed it with his wife and they decided to try and emigrate to Torblit. They went to the Torblit embassy and filled out the appropriate paperwork. They were told decisions can take up to one hundred fifty days.

He was surprised to hear from the Torblit embassy fifteen days later. They wanted him to come in for an interview. He made an appointment for the following day. When Hasin and his wife arrived at the embassy they were taken to small office. The man behind the desk said, "We do not normally allow people to emigrate from Crosus. However, I noticed you were involved in scientific research. What kind of research did you do?"

"I did weapons research and design. I was ordered to design a weapon that would be capable of destroying an entire solar system. I actually completed the design but the process was too slow to be useful. I was ordered to improve the system or my family and I would suffer as a result of my failure. I decided I didn't want to design a weapon that could potentially kill billions of people or put my family at risk. So, I sabotaged the project by destroying the prototype and all the design data except one copy of the data I saved for myself. I had previously sent my wife and our children here so they would be out of the reach of the Crosus government. Now we would like to go someplace where the government of Crosus can't bother us."

"That's quite a story. Can you provide us with any proof that your story is true?"

"I have my copy of the design data for the weapon with me. I sold the ship I was supposed to use to test the prototype as soon as I arrived here. If you have spies on Crosus I'm sure they could verify that I was involved in weapons research."

"If what you have told me is true, all of us in the trade group are in your debt. I'm sure I can verify some of what you told me. Because communication with Crosus is slow that verification may take sixty days. If you are discovered here come back to the embassy and we will give you asylum."

"Thank you, sir. We will be waiting to hear from you."

Hasin and his wife thought the meeting went well, and although they liked Beljang, they both realized they were still in danger. The next forty-two days went by slowly. Each day their concern for their safety grew. Hasin had decided that if he didn't hear from the Torblit embassy within two days he was going to ask them if they could arrange for his children to go there so at least they would be safe. That turned out to be unnecessary. Later that day he received a call from the Torblit embassy asking him and his wife to come in the following morning.

When they arrived at the embassy they were taken to a large conference room. There were several people in the room already. After Hasin and his wife sat down the person at the head of the table stood up and said, "Thank you for coming on such short notice. I'm Portug Freedit, the Torblit Ambassador to Beljang. I want you to know that we were able to verify your background information. We sent that information to Earth. After they reviewed the information they have a proposal for you to consider. Please put on the translators that are on the table in front of you."

The ambassador sat down and the man next to him stood up. "Good morning, my name is Brandon Simpson. I'm in charge of research at NASA. I don't know if you know anything about NASA so I will give you a little background. NASA was founded almost two hundred years ago on Earth in a country called the United States. It originally stood for National Aeronautics and

17

Space Administration. The United States, and several of its neighbors, joined together to become the North American Union. About the same time NASA's mission had changed. It was now only involved in space travel. Now NASA stands for North American Space Administration. NASA developed, with the help of some beings from Procolt 2, the new propulsion and communication systems that are being used everywhere except Crosus. We are in the process of setting up a new research facility on Procolt 2. We would like to offer you a position at that research facility. It will include an excellent salary and free housing for you and your family. I can promise you will be safe there. Procolt 2 is protected by Coplent. Since the last Crosus attack there is a Coplent war ship in orbit around Procolt 2 at all times. Are you interested?"

"Yes, I'm very interested. But do you realize that one of the primary goals of the Crosus government is to destroy Procolt 2?"

"I'm aware of that. We are hoping you can assist us in developing something that will protect Procolt 2 against any weapon Crosus might develop."

"I must tell you I feel I'm responsible for the development of the weapon Crosus planned to use, so I feel compelled to assist you with that type of deterrent. I don't want to develop offensive weapons anymore."

Brandon said, "I'm very glad to hear you say that. The research facility should be completed within a half year, but you are welcome to emigrate to Procolt 2 at any time. Until the facility is completed, you and your family are welcome to stay at Procolt Paradise."

Hasin and his wife looked at each other and smiled. Hasin asked happily, "Can we leave tomorrow?"

"I will be leaving here in two days. You and your family are welcome to travel with me to Procolt 2."

18

"Thank you, sir. We are happy to accept your kind offer."

"You're welcome. Please call me Brandon. My ship is small, so there isn't much room for you to take personal items. Just bring what you will need. Anything else can be acquired on Procolt 2. I'll have someone pick you up and bring you to my ship. Do you have any questions?"

"How long will the trip to Procolt 2 take?"

"Not long, about three days. The distance to Procolt 2 is seventy light years. Is that okay?"

"Yes, of course. I was just curious. Thank you again for your kindness."

"You're welcome. Please keep the translators. I'll have two more on the ship for your children. I'll see you the day after tomorrow."

The meeting broke up and Hasin and his wife went back home. They were both very happy. When their kids heard the news about them moving to Procolt 2 they were happy too, but when they heard they would be living at Procolt Paradise they were absolutely thrilled.

The day they were supposed to leave all of them woke up very early. They had already packed their clothes and a few small personal items in their suitcases. Nobody was hungry so they skipped breakfast. The car arrived to pick them up at 9:00. By 10:30 they were aboard Brandon's ship. When they arrived, Brandon gave them a quick tour of the ship. There were three cabins, each with its own bath. There was also a control room, a kitchen, and a recreation room. It wasn't very big, but Hasin and his family were very pleased with their accommodations.

Once the ship was underway Brandon asked Hasin to come into the recreation room because he wanted to ask him some questions. After they were both seated Brandon said, "Please tell me how this weapon you designed was supposed to work."

"The device is designed to accelerate the sun's aging process and bring it quickly into the 'red giant' stage. Depending on the size of the sun, it could expand enough to engulf any planets within two hundred million units. Our simulations indicated the device will work, but I originally thought the sun would reach its maximum growth within thirty days. It will actually take almost a year. That would give the people on the planet more than enough time to evacuate, and that was unacceptable to the Crosus government."

"Are you absolutely certain Crosus will be unable to develop the weapon now?"

"No, I'm not. I destroyed the prototype and the design data, but it's possible they will start the development process again. The people who assisted me are still there. They probably could start the project over again, and they would have a significant head start because of their existing knowledge."

"How long do you think it would take them to complete the weapon again?"

"I would guess in about two or three years they could be at the point where I destroyed the data and the prototype. But remember, the government insists the weapon must work within thirty days. Neither I nor my assistants have any idea how to do that."

"I don't think we can safely assume they won't figure it out. Do you have any ideas on how we can protect ourselves from the weapon?"

"I've been thinking about that for several days and I have a few ideas."

Brandon and Hasin spent the next two hours discussing possible ways to disable the weapon. Together they came up with a plan, but Brandon said, "We need to discuss this with S12 when we get to Procolt 2. She is a native of Procolt 2. She and I developed the new propulsion and communication systems together. The design was hers. I supplied the knowledge to make the systems a reality. She is, without a doubt, the most intelligent physicist I have ever met. You will be surprised when you see her, but after you talk to her for a few minutes you will be absolutely convinced she is brilliant."

"I don't judge people by their appearance."

"Just remember that when you see her."

They landed at Procolt Paradise three days later. Brandon contacted Jeffery to let him know when they would be arriving and asked Jeffery to bring S12 with him to meet Hasin and his family at the landing pad.

Procolt 2

Jeffery, Debbie, their daughter Mystic, and S12 were all there to greet Brandon and the Tork family. Brandon got off the ship first, followed by Hasin, his wife, and the two children.

Hasin stared at S12, but didn't say anything. Brandon said, "Hi, it's really nice to see all of you again. Mystic, you have really grown since the last time I saw you."

Mystic smiled and said, "Hi, Uncle Brandon. I'm almost four years old now."

Brandon bent down and kissed Mystic lightly on her forehead and said softly, "You're getting to be a big girl."

Mystic giggled.

Then Brandon turned toward S12 and said, "I would like you to meet Hasin Tork, his wife Frazen, and their two children, Altin and Symbit."

Hasin was still staring at S12 when she spoke, "It's a pleasure to meet all of you. Hasin, I'm very anxious to speak to you regarding the weapon you developed for Crosus."

Hasin, stammering, replied, "I'm available at your convenience."

Brandon said, "We'll meet you in the main restaurant in two hours."

S12 responded, "That will be fine." Then she turned around and walked back to the resort.

Debbie said, "Please come with me and I'll show you your new home."

"I'll come to your apartment in 1.75 hours," Brandon added.

Debbie and Mystic guided the Tork family to the Earth guest tower. On the way, they pointed out the amenities the resort offered. They explained everything was included with the apartment which NASA was paying for.

They took the elevator to the fifty-eighth floor. Then Mystic led them to their apartment. As soon as they walked in the entire family smiled. They had never lived in a place as nice as this apartment. The family walked from room to room exploring it together. It had three large bedrooms, four full bathrooms, a large kitchen, a dining room, and a big living room. From the window in the living room they had a beautiful view of the lake and the newly rebuilt marina.

While the Torks were busy getting accustomed to their new home, Jeffery and Brandon went to the restaurant for a cup of coffee. After they sat down Brandon said, "I think we have a reason to be concerned. On the way, I spoke to Hasin about the weapon he developed. He believes, as do I, that even though he destroyed the prototype and the design plans for the weapon, Crosus will eventually be able to build it."

"What does the weapon do?"

"It causes the sun to enter into the red giant phase of its life cycle. That would destroy all the planets within a two hundred million unit orbit around the sun."

"They must really be pissed off at me to want to destroy the whole Procolt System!"

"It's not just you. They want to destroy Earth and Coplent too."

"Does Hasin think he can build something that will counteract the effects of the weapon?"

"Yes, he does. He explained the process to me, and it sounded reasonable. However, I want him to discuss it with S12. I would like to get her opinion."

"I could tell that you never told him S12 was a big squirrel."

"You're right, but I did tell him that he would be surprised by her appearance."

"And he was. Please let me know the results from your meeting this afternoon."

"Of course."

When Brandon knocked on the door of Hasin's apartment, Hasin opened the door almost immediately. He looked at Brandon and asked, "Why didn't you tell me S12 was a rodent?"

"I don't consider her a rodent. I consider her an equal. She may look like an animal, but that's where the resemblance ends," Brandon responded sternly.

"I'm sorry, I didn't mean to offend you or her. I just find it unsettling to speak to her. Do you know why she's so smart? Are there more like her?"

"I do understand how you feel. I felt the same way until I had an opportunity to speak to her. I'm sure you will feel better about working with her after our meeting. The reason she is so smart is there's some type of radiation on the surface of this planet that affects living organisms with a specific type of DNA. For squirrels, it affected them physically and mentally. They have developed hands with opposable thumbs, their life spans have increased substantially, and they have developed the ability to use more of their brain than any other living creature. They also have one other really unique capability. Their offspring have all the knowledge of their parents. S12 has not had any children, but if she does her children will be born with all her knowledge. I think the squirrel population is about one hundred. Jeffery built a home for them called 'Squirrel Haven'."

"Okay, let's go to our meeting."

Brandon and Hasin went to the restaurant and found S12 was already there waiting for them. After Brandon and Hasin were seated, S12 said, "Hasin, I realize you find it uncomfortable speaking to a squirrel. I've noticed this many times in my interactions with humanoids and I'm not offended. I hope after we have spent some time together you will be more comfortable with the situation."

"Just hearing you say that already makes me more comfortable. Have you had an opportunity to look at the plans for the weapon?" Hasin asked.

"Yes, it took a while because at first I was unable to read your language. I sent a message to Coplent asking them to send some language learning material so I could learn it. It took me two days to learn, so now I have no problem reading the material. The design is most impressive, and I have an idea of how we might be able to terminate the reaction if we find out about it within ten days. After that, it may be unstoppable."

Hasin looked at S12 and removed his translator. S12 removed hers as well. It was obvious Hasin intended to test S12's ability to speak Crosus. Then Hasin asked, "What two elements are used to cause the primary reaction?"

S12 responded, in perfect Crosus, "The two primary elements used to cause the reaction are platinum and carbon. Did I pass your test?"

"Yes, you passed the test. I'll never doubt you again. Please forgive me. It was very rude of me to do that," Hasin said meekly.

"I understand, but there is nothing to forgive. However, you need to use the translator so Brandon can participate in the discussion."

Hasin put his translator back on. They spent the next three hours discussing different methods for terminating the reaction. At the end of the discussion they had a plan. Hasin was going to build a computer simulation of the weapon while Brandon and S12 worked on a series of tests to evaluate several different methods to terminate the weapon's reaction.

S12 went home to Squirrel Haven while Brandon and Hasin went to Hasin's apartment. As they stepped into the elevator Brandon asked, "What is your opinion of S12 now?"

"I believe her participation in this project greatly enhances the likelihood that we will be successful. She is, without question, the most intelligent scientist I have ever met."

"I'm very happy to hear you say that. I feel exactly the same way. The laboratory facility won't be completed for at least one hundred fifty days, so I'm going to ask Jeffery if we can use one of the empty apartments as our lab until the facility is completed. I'll also order all the equipment we will need. I think we should be able to get started in ten days."

"So, I have some time to enjoy the place with my family for a while. That's wonderful! We have never had an opportunity like this before. I don't have the words to tell you how grateful I am."

The elevator stopped, and as Hasin stepped out Brandon said, "I'm glad you're happy, but when the temporary lab is ready your vacation will be over."

Hasin looked back over his shoulder and said, "I know, but I'm looking forward to working with you and S12 too."

It took almost a year for Hasin, S12, and Brandon to find a way to terminate the actions of the Crosus weapon. All the computer simulations indicated it would work, but they had no way to test it. Now Hasin wished he hadn't sent the prototype to the planet in the Lundalt system. It was a gas giant and he could not think of any way to retrieve it, but he decided to ask Brandon and S12 anyway.

"We need to find a way to test our theory with a real weapon. There are two possibilities. We could build one, which would probably take one hundred fifty days, or we could retrieve the prototype weapon that I sent to the planet in the Lundalt System. The weapon sends out a homing signal which would enable us to locate it, but I have no idea how to retrieve it. Do either of you have any ideas?"

"Since the planet is a gas giant it probably has fairly low gravity at higher altitudes. If the weapon is in the upper atmosphere we might be able to retrieve it with a ship and the transporter system Coplent uses," Brandon responded.

S12 was silent for a minute then she said, "I think the range of the Coplent transporter is only about five units. I believe the plan would work if we could increase the effective range to five hundred units. Brandon, can you get me the plans for the device?"

"I'm sure I can have them here in two or three days. I'll send a message to Coplent today. Do you think that modifying the transporter design will be faster than building a duplicate of the weapon?"

"Until I have had a chance to study the plans I don't know if it will be faster, but I feel it will be safer. I don't want to build a weapon that powerful."

Hasin said, "I understand how you feel. If we built it and Crosus found out, they could try to steal it. A small band of Crosus soldiers could easily land here undetected by the Coplent warship that is in orbit to protect us."

Brandon said, "I agree. Let's try to retrieve the prototype."

Crosus

Bejort Griss and Jensor Kiltor were seated at a table in Bejort's office. Jensor said, "Sir, I'm sure you're aware that Hasin Tork should have returned from the Lundalt system by now. He was due back more than thirty days ago. I think we must assume his mission was a failure."

"You are correct, of course, but I don't like the idea of starting over with the weapons design. I find it difficult to believe the plans for the weapon and Hasin are both gone."

"Sir, I think Hasin's team could rebuild the weapon in less than two years. Even though the plans were lost, they are certain they can duplicate the last prototype."

"Okay, get them started on it immediately. I also want a team to try to duplicate the communication system the trade group is using. We've lost a year because our communication is too slow to be useful."

"We have some information regarding the communication system. We were able to obtain a unit on Beljang. It doesn't appear to be that complex. I think we may be able to duplicate it in less than a year."

"I'm counting on it. You know the consequences for failure."

"Yes sir, I do. I won't fail."

Procolt 2

After the meeting with Hasin and S12, Brandon wondered if the Coplent Warship had a copy of the plans for the transporter. He contacted the commander of the ship and asked about it. The commander told him he would have the plans sent immediately. Brandon had them a few moments later. He called S12 and she walked over to the Development Lab immediately.

She sat at a low table that was specifically built for her and began studying the plans. About an hour later she said, "Brandon, I believe the range of the unit is limited only by the amount of power supplied to it. It was designed to work with a minimal drain of the ship's power system. However, we don't have any limitations on available power. I believe we can increase the range to two hundred units by simply altering the power supply."

"Do you think that will be enough to allow us to retrieve Hasin's prototype?"

"Since we don't have any idea where the prototype is located, I can't answer the question. If they have a spare transporter on the warship I think we can modify it in a few days."

"I'll contact them and find out if they have a spare unit."

Brandon walked into his small office and called the warship's commander. The commander was very excited about the possibility of extending the range of the transporter. He told Brandon there were two spare units on board, and he would have one brought down to the surface immediately.

Brandon went back into the work area and said, "We'll have a transporter here within two hours."

S12 responded excitedly, "Perfect! I'll start working on modifying a power module immediately."

The transporter was modified and ready for testing two days later. Brandon took a small tool box with him and drove one of the resort's all-terrain vehicles to about twenty units north of the

29

resort. He stopped and contacted S12. She turned on the viewer that was part of the transporter system and locked onto the signal from Brandon's communicator. She used the viewer to locate the toolbox and activated the transporter. A few seconds later the toolbox was a few feet from her, in the lab.

When Brandon returned to the lab S12 said, "The test at twenty units was perfect. Let's try it at two hundred."

Brandon picked up the toolbox and said, "I'll take this to my ship and call you in about .2 hours." Then he left the lab and went to his ship that was parked about a half unit away. He flew the ship to a location two hundred seven units west of the resort. After landing in a large meadow, he contacted S12 again to tell her he was ready. A few seconds later the toolbox disappeared. Then Brandon received a call from S12. After Brandon answered she said, "The test was not successful. The toolbox was destroyed. It actually looks like it was melted. I need to look at the plans again."

"Okay, I'll head back to the lab. I'm sure we can resolve this problem fairly quickly."

When Brandon got back to the lab, S12 and Hasin were both studying the transporter plans. Brandon joined them and they spent the next six hours analyzing the plans. Hasin thought he had a solution to the problem. He felt the toolbox image was lost because there was no actual receiving device. He suggested they design a receiver that would be able to detect weaker signals. S12 and Brandon agreed.

It took three days to design the receiver and two weeks to build it because they needed parts from Coplent. When it was completed they tested it with items in the resort. It seemed to work perfectly. Brandon picked up a small plastic box and said, "I'll go to the same spot where it failed before."

When he landed he contacted S12 and she activated the transporter. This time it worked perfectly. On his way out, Brandon had grabbed a container of coffee from the restaurant. It was empty now and sitting in a holder next to his seat. Brandon called S12 again.

"I'm going to go five hundred units above the resort. There is an empty coffee container you can use for the test." The test at five hundred units was also successful. That meant they were ready to try to retrieve the prototype weapon.

They decided to leave as soon as the transporter was installed in Brandon's ship. Four days later they were ready to go. Brandon contacted Jeffery and told him they were leaving. Jeffery wished them good luck and went to the shuttle port because a group from Earth was scheduled to arrive in .5 hours.

Jeffery or Debbie greeted every group that arrived and it was Jeffery's turn. As the people stepped off the ship he smiled at them and directed them to the check-in desk in the lobby.

Lundalt System

Brandon's ship was in orbit above the only planet in the Lundalt system. Hasin had already programmed the ship's computer to scan for the signal generated by the weapon. The ship was fifty thousand units above the atmosphere of the planet. At that distance they would be able to scan about eleven percent of the area. Each scan took several hours, so they did not expect to find the weapon anytime soon.

On the third scan the weapon was located. It was deeper in the atmosphere than they hoped. The gravity at that altitude was almost three times the surface gravity on Procolt 2. In order to retrieve the weapon they would have to place Brandon's ship in a parallel orbit a hundred units higher than the weapon. Their velocity would have to be slightly faster than the weapon, and that presented a problem. If they were traveling faster than the weapon their altitude would increase. In order for the plan to work, the speed and altitude of the ship had to be controlled with extreme precision.

They had two other problems as well. Ships like Brandon's only required the use of their conventional propulsion system for landing, takeoff, and maneuvering the ship in space. The ship only had enough fuel for a single attempt. After transporting the weapon on board, there would only be enough fuel to increase their orbital speed enough that they would be free of the planet's gravitational pull in about thirty hours. After they got back to Procolt 2 they would have to get help from the Coplent warship above the planet in order to land. The other problem was, once they were inside the planet's atmosphere it was probable the communication system would not function correctly.

They spent the next day running simulations with the ship's computer. The last simulation indicated an eighty-three percent chance of success. It also indicated that even if they managed to

32

successfully transport the weapon to the ship there was a thirty percent chance they would not have enough fuel to escape the planet's gravity.

Brandon sent a message to Jeffery telling him their plan. The message also said that if Jeffery did not receive another message within thirty-six hours he should send a ship to rescue them.

They had to wait three hours before the weapon would be in the correct position for the plan to work. The piloting of the ship was being done by computer, so they could only wait and see what happens. Once they were close enough to the weapon the transporter would be activated manually. They only had one pass. After the ship passed the position of the weapon it would begin to accelerate and bring them out of orbit.

Two minutes before the maneuver was to start each of them took their seats. S12 was seated at the console that controlled the transporter. Her display also showed the position of the weapon relative to the ship. They would enter an orbit around the planet twenty thousand units behind the weapon and one hundred units above it. The ships speed was five thousand units per hour faster than the orbital speed of the weapon. The ship would be in range to transport the weapon twenty minutes after entering orbit for about one minute.

The ship bounced around as it entered the desired orbit, then a few moments later the ride smoothed out. S12's monitor indicated that the weapon was slightly more than nineteen thousand units ahead and one hundred seven units below their path.

The plan was to launch a small probe containing a transporter receiver at the weapon. The probe contained a very strong magnet which would attach itself to the weapon if it was less than ten feet away. S12 studied the signal from the weapon and said, "We won't need the receiver. I'm sure I can program the transporter to use the signal from the weapon instead." It took her less than ten minutes to modify the transporter's program.

Eight minutes later the weapon was one hundred seventy units in front of them. S12 watched the monitor and when it indicated they had closed the horizontal distance to less than one hundred units she activated the transporter. Thirty seconds later the weapon was on the bridge. The transporter automatically shut off after the transport was complete.

As they passed the position where the weapon had been, the ships engines turned on. Brandon watched as their velocity increased. In thirteen seconds the ship speed would be sufficient to escape the planet's gravitational pull. Unfortunately, the engine ran out of fuel two seconds too soon. They were trapped in an orbit around the planet.

Procolt 2

S37 had been trained to operate the communication system. When he received the message from Brandon about the plan to retrieve the weapon he contacted Jeffery immediately.

Jeffery was sitting in the restaurant with Debbie and Mystic having lunch when he received the message. After S37 read the message Jeffery thanked him and closed his com unit. Then he said, "Debbie, would you be interested in a quick trip to the Lundalt system?"

With more than a little concern in her voice she asked, "What's wrong?"

"Maybe nothing. I won't know for sure for another thirty-six hours. Brandon, Hasin, and S12 found the weapon they were searching for, but it was not in an easily accessible location. They were going to try to retrieve it, but there was a substantial possibility they would end up in orbit around the planet and not have sufficient fuel to escape."

"If that happens how are we going to rescue them? The transporters don't work with living things."

"I think we will have to dock with them and use our ship to carry them out of orbit."

"That's never been done before. Are you sure it will work?"

"I'm not absolutely certain, but I don't see any reason why it wouldn't. We don't have to accelerate from zero, so the strain on the docking mechanism would be minimal. Anyway, I'll discuss this with S1. I'm sure one of the squirrels will have the answer. But this is all theoretical at the moment. I'm hoping the rescue mission won't be necessary, but I want to be prepared."

"This will be a dangerous mission. If you have to go take Brealak with you. I don't want Mystic to be an orphan."

"I understand. I asked you if you wanted to go, but I never had any intention of putting us both in harm's way."

Jeffery used his communicator and asked S1 and Brealak to come to the restaurant immediately. Both of them arrived ten minutes later. Jeffery explained the situation. Brealak immediately agreed to accompany Jeffery on the mission. S1 said he would discuss the technical aspects of Jeffery's plan with some of the other squirrels immediately.

An hour later S1 contacted Jeffery and told him that the docking mechanism would have to be modified slightly to handle the strain unless the level of acceleration was kept below two units per minute. Jeffery thought for a few moments and then responded that the limitation would be acceptable.

The next day Jeffery and Brealak spent two hours preparing a ship in case a rescue was required. There was about twelve hours left before the thirty-six hour time limit would elapse and the closer that time came the more Jeffery was concerned about the mission.

An hour before the time limit expired Jeffery was sitting in his apartment with Debbie. Every few minutes Jeffery looked at his watch to see how much time was left. Debbie noticed what he was doing and asked, "Why are you so nervous about this rescue mission?"

"I've been wondering about that myself. I know the mission is dangerous, but I've been on dangerous missions before and I never felt this way. I'm concerned I may not be coming back. If that happens please tell Mystic as she grows up how much I love her."

"That won't be necessary because I'm sure you're coming back and you can tell her how much you love her yourself. You are usually very self-confident. I think the reason you're so concerned is because you're now responsible for someone besides yourself."

36

"You're probably right, but that doesn't make me feel any better about the mission."

"Consider this; you and Brealak are probably among the most experienced pilots in the trade group. Other than the docking maneuver, you have done all this before many times. I'm sure the docking maneuver will be done by the ship's computer. All you have to do is watch."

"I know all that, but I'm still worried."

They continued to talk for a while. Then Debbie looked at her watch and said softly, "It's time to go."

Jeffery walked over to Debbie, smiled at her, and then kissed her goodbye. Mystic was taking a nap so he walked quietly into her bedroom. He watched her sleep for a minute and thought about how much he loved her. Then he bent down and kissed her goodbye too.

Fifteen minutes later he walked into the ship they would be using for the rescue mission. Brealak was already on board. When she saw Jeffery she said, "They finished installing the auxiliary fuel tank about an hour ago and both tanks are full. We are all set to go."

Jeffery didn't respond immediately. Brealak noticed the look of concern on his face and she asked, "What's wrong?"

"I have a bad feeling about this mission. Debbie told me not to worry. She assured me the two of us can take care of any problem that arises, but I'm still worried."

"If I had to make a guess why you are so concerned I'll bet it would be because of Mystic."

"You're right. Debbie and I just discussed it a few minutes ago. If everything is ready, let's go."

"Okay, take your seat and we will be on our way in two minutes."

Lundalt System

The trip to the Lundalt system was uneventful. Brealak put the ship into an orbit thirty thousand units above the atmosphere of the planet and began scanning for Brandon's ship. Three hours later Brealak said excitedly, "I found it!"

"That's great! How close do you think we will have to be for our com units to work?"

"According to the computer the atmospheric conditions are not conducive to radio frequency transmissions. I would guess we would have to be less than three thousand units from their ship."

"Give me the information you have regarding their orbit and I'll program the computer to get us in com range. I think we'll have to maneuver manually to within .25 units of their ship before we can begin the docking procedure."

Brealak printed out the position report generated by the ship's computer and handed it to Jeffery. He spent the next hour programming the computer and running simulations. When he was satisfied with the results he said, "We have to wait for about four hours before their ship will be in the proper position to start our rendezvous."

The time seemed to go by quickly. Everything would be done automatically so Jeffery and Brealak watched the external monitor. From this distance above the planet it looked beautiful. There were numerous breaks in the cloud cover and through those openings they could see red, orange, and yellow patterns. They were both watching when the computer announced that the maneuver would begin in .025 hours.

They felt the increase in gravity as the ship began the descent into the planet's atmosphere. The ship began to bounce around as it was buffeted by a combination of the atmosphere and the increased gravity from the planet. They both watched the monitor as it showed the distance to Brandon's ship decrease.

When it indicated the ships were less than three thousand units apart Jeffery tried to contact Brandon.

Brandon answered, "Hi Jeffery, thank you for coming to rescue us. I guess you got our message."

"Yes, Brealak and I are about three thousand units behind you. I'm going to maneuver my ship to within .1 units of yours and then we will begin the docking procedure."

"What happens after we are docked?"

"We will begin to accelerate slowly until we reach escape velocity. I didn't want to wait for modifications to be made to the docking mechanism so we have to limit our acceleration to 2 units per hour. At that rate it will take about one hundred two hours to reach the speed we need."

"Okay, we don't have any fuel to move the ship so you will have to do it all on your own."

"I assumed that when I programmed the computer to do the maneuver. I'll contact you again when we are close enough to start the docking procedure."

"Okay, we'll talk again soon."

An hour later Brandon's ship was visible on the short-range monitor. Brealak contacted Brandon and she described what was happening. The computer was displaying how far Jeffery's ship was from the optimum position to begin the procedure. It was a slow, painstaking process. Almost an hour had passed until the computer indicated the ships were properly aligned. Then the computer took over. The docking procedure went smoothly and .25 hours later the ships were locked together.

Jeffery began the acceleration process. The passengers on both ships felt the slight increase in gravity and everyone was relieved. Now all they could do was wait until they were out of reach on the planet's gravity. With each hour, the pull of the planet was noticeably reduced as the increase in speed caused the height of their orbit to increase.

Just as the computer calculated, one hundred two hours after the acceleration started they were free of the planet's gravitational pull. Enough fuel was transferred to Brandon's ship so he would be able to land when he returned to Procolt 2. The ships undocked and .15 hours later Brandon's ship began the journey to Procolt 2. A few minutes later Brealak programmed the computer to take them home. The mission was a complete success. Brealak looked at Jeffery, smiled, and said, "I told you that you had nothing to worry about."

Both ships arrived at Procolt 2 three days later. Debbie and Mystic were there to meet Jeffery as he stepped off the ship. He hugged and kissed them both. Then the three of them, and Brealak, went to the restaurant to get some real food.

When Brandon's ship landed Brandon called the maintenance department and asked them to bring the weapon to his lab. Then Brandon and Hasin went to the restaurant and S12 went home to Squirrel Haven.

The next morning Brandon, Hasin, and S12 were in their lab. S12 arrived a few hours before the others and she spent the time studying the weapon. By the time the others arrived she had completed her analysis. She said, "After examining the weapon I'm certain that in addition to our plan to restore a star to normal after it has been exposed to the weapon, I believe we may be able to prevent the device from activating at all if we bombard it with high energy radio waves. It takes about twenty hours for the process to begin, but the components are not well shielded, so the high energy radio frequency radiation will destroy many of the components rendering the weapon useless."

Hasin said softly, "I should have thought about that possibility myself. I'm sorry. But if we want to test that we'll have to build a duplicate of the control system."

"I'm positive we can do that, if we can get identical components," S12 responded.

"Hasin, please get me a list of components and I'll order them from Coplent," Brandon requested.

"I'll have it for you in two hours. But nothing can be substituted. They must be identical."

"I understand, but that may not be possible since I can't order them from a supplier on Crosus."

Hasin nodded his head to indicate he understood the problem. Then he said, "Now that we have the weapon here we have to start building the device we believe will neutralize it. We should start on that immediately.

S12 said, "I agree. We already know what the device has to do, and I have been thinking about the design for a while. I should have the plans completed in day or two. I don't think it will take more than three months to build."

The Crosus weapon worked by producing radiation that would exponentially increase the fusion reactions in the star. That would increase the energy released inside the star, and the increased energy would cause an even greater increase in the level of fusion. The only way to halt the self-destructing actions in the star was to first eliminate the radiation being generated by the weapon and then flood the star with heavier elements that would bind with the hydrogen atoms. As these heavier elements dispersed through the star, the level of fusion reactions would slow down because there would be less free hydrogen to fuel them.

One of the biggest problems with the device they had to build was to make it so it would be able to withstand the surface temperatures on the star, but Hasin had already developed that part of the technology.

Ten days later the parts to build a duplicate control system for the Crosus weapon arrived. So did some of the components that were needed to build their star-saving device. Hasin worked on building the control system while Brandon and S12 worked on the other project.

Hasin's task was much easier, and he had the control system completed in eight days. He tested the completed control system to make sure it functioned correctly. When he verified it was functioning, S12 began building the device that would destroy it.

Because there was a possibility that the destruction of the control system would cause an explosion or a fire, they decided to perform the test away from Procolt Paradise. Brandon loaded the equipment needed and they flew a hundred units north of the resort.

Hasin and S12 set up the test while Brandon watched. When all was ready Hasin powered on the control system. Then S12 turned on the high-power radio frequency signal generator she designed. Almost instantly the control system failed. A second later it began to crackle and then it burst into flames. The test was a complete success, and further evidence of S12's ability to analyze and resolve problems quickly and correctly the first time.

After the test was finished Brandon said, "I'm glad we did the test here. I think Jeffery would have been upset if we set fire to our lab." Then looking at S12 he asked, "Do you think there is some way to create a defense system with this technology?"

S12 looked thoughtful, or at least as thoughtful as a squirrel can look, for several seconds. Then she said, "I think it's possible, but I'm not sure it's practical. I'll have to think about it for a while."

Hasin said, "If we could create a defense system it would be unnecessary to build a star-saving device."

S12 responded, "I'm not sure about that. Unless the defense system is one hundred percent foolproof, there is still a possibility the Crosus weapon could hit a star, and I don't believe any defense system could be perfect.

Brandon said, "S12 is correct Hasin. We still have to build the Star Saver."

42

"I like that name, we should call it the Star Saver instead of just calling it the device," S12 added.

"I like that too," Hasin said.

For the next several weeks Hasin and Brandon worked on the Star Saver, while S12 worked on the defense system. During that time S12 hardly said a word to Brandon or Hasin. She immediately rebuffed any attempt at conversation. She was constantly deep in thought.

Then one morning everything changed. When Brandon arrived at the lab S12 was already there. She said cheerfully, "Good morning Brandon, it's going to be a wonderful day!"

"It's nice to see you talking again. Hasin and I were both very worried about you."

"I know and I'm sorry, but sometimes when I'm thinking about a complex subject I have to block out everything else. However, I figured out how to build the defense system."

"That's great! Would you like to explain it to me?"

"The basic problem was how to flood the area around a star with high energy radio waves. I was trying to figure out a way to transmit a signal that would cover the surface of the star we were trying to protect. Once I realized it would be impossible to do that I started thinking about other options. What I thought about was the original idea you had to utilize drones traveling between relay stations that were one light year apart for a high-speed communication system. All we have to do is build a drone capable of traveling around a star in a series of circles. The circles would be about a thousand units apart. Each orbital pass would be completed in a fraction of a second and we would be able to cover the entire surface of the star like Procolt in less than two seconds. The drone would constantly blast the area around it with the appropriate radio waves. I am certain I can make a transmitter that will have an effective range of a thousand units so each pass would overlap with the previous pass."

43

"Yes, that's a great idea! Since the weapon has to travel slow enough that it won't be destroyed on impact, I'm positive your plan will work."

"I can have a prototype ready to test in sixty days. Then we can deploy it around Procolt and test it with dummy weapons."

"I think we should concentrate on this and put the Star Saver on hold for a while."

"I suppose we can do that, but you know the risk."

"I do, and I think the risk is minimal for now. Once this defense system is deployed around Procolt we can go back to working on the Star Saver."

"Once we validate that it works on Procolt, we will have to install it in the Coplent system and around Earth's sun as well."

Just at that moment Hasin walked into the lab. He saw Brandon and S12 and immediately realized that S12 was out of her depression. He said, "S12, it's nice to see you happy again. What's going on?"

S12 explained the defense system to Hasin. Like Brandon, he thought it was a great idea. They started work on it that day. They decided to call the device they were building the Star Defender.

Brandon thought S12's estimate of sixty days was probably a little optimistic, but with all three of them working on the project it was actually ready two days ahead of schedule.

Hasin built three more control systems and mounted them in disposable probes. They loaded the drones and the Star Defender on Brandon's ship and moved into an orbit halfway between Procolt 1 and the Procolt sun. The computer on the Star Defender had been programmed with the orbital requirements and they launched it. The Star Defender had a small tachyon propulsion system and was traveling at about thirty times light speed in just a few seconds. They waited for an hour watching the Star Defender to be sure it was in the correct orbit. Since the system was passive,

44

all they had to do was launch a probe at Procolt and see what happens.

Hasin adjusted the probe to travel at one hundred thousand units per hour and launched it. At that speed, it would take about three hours before the probe would pass the orbit of the Star Defender.

They were all watching the monitor as the probe approached the critical orbit. As it passed through the orbit it exploded. Then they tried the two remaining probes launching them only a few minutes apart. They were destroyed too.

Brandon believed the mission to eliminate the threat posed by Crosus had been successfully completed.

Within three hundred days the Star Defender had been installed in the solar systems of every major member of the trade group. During that time Brandon, Hasin, and S12 completed the design of the Star Saver and built a prototype. They planned to test it in the Lundalt system within thirty days.

The Squirrels

The test of the Star Saver was successful. Three days after Brandon, Hasin, and S12 returned something happened that had a profound effect on the squirrel population.

Jeffery, Debbie, and Mystic were having breakfast in the restaurant when S12 walked up to their table. She looked sad, but before Jeffery had a chance to ask her what was wrong she said sadly, "I'm sorry to inform you that S1 died last night."

No one said anything for a few seconds. Then Jeffery said, "I'm sorry to hear that. I always considered him a friend." Jeffery paused for another moment and continued, "Actually, he was much more than a friend, he was part of our family. He will be missed by all of us."

Mystic began to cry and Debbie did her best to comfort her. It was the first time Mystic had to deal with the death of someone she knew.

S12 said, "We would like your help. His death is the first that has occurred since you arrived here. Our old method of dealing with a death is no longer appropriate for us. I've read about how humans hold funeral services when one of you dies, but we have never had any experience doing that. Could you arrange something for us?"

Debbie responded, "Yes, of course. I'll be happy to do that for you. Do you know what you want to do with his body?"

"When we lived in the caves and one of us died, we took the body out of the cave and placed it in a shallow grave that we dug in one of the meadows. But now that just doesn't seem right. We have no religion, and we don't believe in God, or in life after death as many humans do. However, we would like his body to be placed in a location where we can erect some kind of monument to commemorate his life."

"I understand, and I'm sure we can do that for you," Debbie responded.

"Thank you. We are holding a meeting of all the adult squirrels tonight. We need to find a new leader."

"Please express our condolences to all the squirrels at the meeting. If any of them are scheduled to work, please let them know they are free to attend the meeting instead of working."

"I'll do that. Thank you for your help," S12 said. Then she turned around and walked in the direction of Squirrel Haven.

Debbie spent the afternoon arranging the goodbye ceremony for S1. She also ordered a small coffin from Earth and arranged for a grave to be dug near Squirrel Haven. She wanted to have some kind of grave marker made as well, but she hesitated because she felt he should have a name, not a number.

The next morning S12 called Jeffery to set up a meeting with him. He said he was in his office with Debbie and now would be the perfect time for a meeting. S12 said she would there in a few minutes.

When S12 arrived at Jeffery's office she walked in, said "Good Morning," and climbed up on a chair.

Debbie said, "Good Morning S12. How did the meeting go last night?"

"The meeting went very well. A lot of decisions were made. That's what I wanted to talk to you about. Probably the most important decision we made was for each of us to have names instead of numbers. We want our civilization to mimic the social structure humans use. At the meeting it was decided that each squirrel would have a last name that corresponded to the job they do. In family groups the job of the lead male in the group would be used for all the family members. Each squirrel could choose their own first name."

"Did the group pick a name for S1? I wanted to have a name on his grave marker, not a number."

47

"Yes, they did. They selected the name George Leader for him. My name is Jessica Teacher. Name tag necklaces are going to be made for every squirrel, except the infants. The group also decided that the most intelligent adult should be the leader of the squirrels. Since they considered me to be the most intelligent, I was selected. We also decided that the Leader would retain the position until they either died, resigned, or were no longer capable of leading the group."

Jeffery asked, "Are you going to continue assisting us with the product development?"

"Yes, for now. However, the squirrel population is growing. There are now two hundred thirty-six of us. As that number grows I may have to spend most of my time handling the responsibilities as Leader. On a personal note, my friend S31, whose name is now Glen Baker, and I are going to become a family group. I want to have a child. Once that child becomes an adult, he or she will take my place in product development."

"Will your name change to Jessica Baker?" Debbie asked.

"Yes, when my child is born. I have to go now and help prepare the Star Saver test, but I wanted to let you know about the results of the meeting."

"Thank you, Jessica," Jeffery said.

Jessica said, "You're welcome," and left the office.

Debbie ordered the grave marker. George Leader's body was taken to Earth to be embalmed. It would be back in ten days and would be shipped with the grave marker. The service for George was scheduled two days after the delivery.

When the new marina was built a banquet hall was included in the design. The hall had been used frequently for parties and weddings, but this would be the first time there would be a memorial service held there.

A burial site was selected near the main entrance to Squirrel Haven. The resort maintenance people dug the grave and mounted the eight foot tall grave marker the day before the service.

Jeffery was scheduled to speak first at the service. He arrived with Debbie and Mystic about ten minutes early. The hall was already filled with mourners. All the squirrels were given the day off, and every one of them was there in a show of respect for George. Most of the resort staff were in attendance as well.

At exactly ten o'clock the lights in the hall dimmed and everyone became silent. Jeffery walked up to the podium. There was some brief applause and then Jeffery began to speak.

"When we first arrived here, almost eight standard years ago, we never expected to find any intelligent beings. The very first time we observed the squirrels we knew we were wrong. We realized immediately that the squirrels had a language and had developed a society. It was another half year before we realized how intelligent they are. As our interactions with the squirrels increased it became obvious we needed a primary contact. George Leader, then known as S1, assumed that position."

"Over the years we worked together, became friends, and then, despite the obvious physical differences, we became more. Now all of the full time residents of Procolt 2 are one big family. That means we love and care about each other and help others whenever it is needed. Although most of us are from either Earth or Coplent, our family has people from twenty-seven of the trade group planets. Today we all mourn George Leader."

"George's finest moment was when we were faced with a potential disaster caused by two terrorists from Crosus. After they destroyed the marina they sent me a list of demands and threatened to kill thousands if I failed to comply. George, using an ability he had kept secret until that time, located the terrorists and put them into a sleep state which enabled us to capture them before they could do any further damage. The two terrorists are still in prison on Earth."

"At this point I would like to turn this memorial service over to Jessica Teacher, formerly known as S12."

Jeffery left the stage and Jessica went to the podium. A stool had been placed behind it, so she climbed up and stood on the stool. She was now high enough to make eye contact with the people in attendance. There was some applause and when it stopped she began to speak. She talked about things Jeffery knew nothing about. What George did to organize them and how he helped them overcome some of the problems they faced as their society grew. She said he was their first teacher, and he was the first squirrel to learn English. Then she spent some time recounting events that George played a critical role in over the years. Finally she said, "George was an exceptional leader and it will be impossible for me to fully replace him, but as your new Leader I will do my best to make this difficult time a little easier for all of us."

Then they all walked to the grave where George would be buried and watched as his little coffin was lowered into the ground. Many of the humans cried, and although squirrels are unable to cry, their sadness was obvious.

Procolt City

Ten days after the burial of George Leader, Jeffery received a note from one of his guests, Oscar Goodman, requesting a meeting with him. Jeffery contacted Oscar and asked to meet him at his office at three o'clock.

At exactly three o'clock a man appeared at the door to Jeffery's office. Jeffery looked up at him and the man smiled. Then he said, "Good afternoon Admiral Whitestone. Thank you for seeing me."

"Please come in. I'm no longer an admiral, and please call me Jeffery. We are very informal here. How can I help you?"

Oscar walked in and sat down across from Jeffery. Then he said, "Jeffery, it's a pleasure to meet you. I represent a group of people from a small city in central Kansas. We have all been here on vacation for the past month and we have a proposal we would like you to consider."

"Okay Oscar, I'm listening."

"We have noticed that every other day a supply ship arrives with commodities that are needed to keep Procolt Paradise running. The primary part of every shipment is food. I'm positive shipping food from Earth or Coplent is very expensive. Is that correct?"

Jeffery thought he knew where this conversation was going. He responded, "Yes, shipping food is very expensive."

"Have you ever thought about growing your own food on Procolt, instead of paying to have it shipped?"

"Yes, I've thought about that frequently. But nobody here has the knowledge or the desire to become a farmer."

"I would like to change all that. Our group is made up of farmers, tradesmen, shopkeepers, and others and we all have one common desire. We all want to leave Earth and move someplace less crowded where we can live a simpler life. We all love it here

51

on Procolt 2 and want to make it our home. We can build the farms and within two years supply you with most of the food you will need. That would benefit all of us."

"I haven't been to Earth for a long time. Has it changed?"

"It's beginning to look more like Coplent every day. The population is now more than twenty billion. Many of the largest cities have banned private vehicles. There are too many people, even the national parks in the United States are overcrowded. Right now, the earliest I could get a reservation at any park is three years away."

"How many people are in your group?"

"Our group here is fifty-four, but we represent about two thousand people."

"It sounds to me like you want to build a small city."

"Yes, that's exactly what we want to do. We are prepared to sell everything we have on Earth, come here, and start a new city. But we can't do it without your approval, and some initial financial assistance. Any financial assistance would be repaid once we start producing the food supplies you need."

"Oscar, that's a very intriguing proposal. When do you return to Earth?"

"We have fifteen more days here."

"I must tell you it has been bothering me for some time that everything we need we have to buy from Earth or Coplent. I'm sure you were here for the memorial service for George, the leader of the squirrels. I had to send his body back to Earth to have it embalmed and I had to order his coffin from Earth as well. That situation made me realize how dependent we are on others, and I think that should change. Can you provide me with a list of the people who want to relocate here and their professions?"

"I'm sure I can have that for you tomorrow. Would you like to meet at three again?"

"Sure, I'll have Debbie and Jim Roberts here too. Jim is in charge of maintenance and construction here. We can discuss what you will need to get started. If we agree to do this you must pick a location for your new city before you return to Earth. While you are gone we can construct some temporary housing for you and your people to use until permanent structures can be built.

"Thank you, Jeffery. This means a lot to us and I promise we won't let you down."

"Okay, I'll see you tomorrow at three, Oscar."

That evening at diner he discussed the proposal with Debbie. Like Jeffery, she thought it was a great idea. Then Jeffery called Jim Roberts and told him about the proposal and the meeting.

The next afternoon at three Oscar showed up at Jeffery's office. Jeffery smiled and waved him in. Debbie and Jim were already there, seated at a small conference table. Oscar sat down and pushed a memory card over to Jeffery. Jeffery took it and made the appropriate introductions. Then Jeffery asked, "Does this contain the information I requested yesterday?"

"Actually, it has more. There is a brief biography of every adult who wants to relocate here by family group. The list includes children who will be coming as well."

"How many total people are involved?"

"There are two thousand seventy-four people. Four of the women are pregnant, so the number may increase slightly before we relocate."

"Are you aware of the radiation here on Procolt 2 and how it affects humans?"

"I've heard rumors about some unusual radiation, but no specifics. Apparently, it isn't harmful or you wouldn't be here."

"You're correct, of course. In actuality, the radiation is beneficial. I will explain the details after we have an agreement."

53

"Okay, by the way, one of the people who will be coming is Craig Whitman. Craig is now a farmer, but he did own a funeral home and is an experienced embalmer."

"I hope we won't need his services for a long time, but I suppose it's good to know we have somebody with that capability. Do you have a plan of what you want to do? I don't want more than two thousand people to suddenly show up here with no place to go."

"Yes, the plan is on that memory card as well. To begin with, about one hundred of us will come here. Many of them have experience in construction. They will build the structures required for phase one. When the structures are finished another two hundred will come and phase two will begin. These people will set up the farms and begin construction of single family homes. They will also build stores, offices, and roads. When phase two is complete the rest of the people will come. We plan on raising cattle and pigs as well as fruits and vegetables."

Jeffery thought about telling him that raising the animals could be a problem because they had the potential to become intelligent, but he decided not to mention it at this time. Instead he said, "I'll go over your plan this evening."

Jim said, "Jeffery, I could build a temporary structure that would be able to house three hundred people in about thirty-five days. That way they could bring three hundred people initially."

"Do you have everything you need to build it?" Jeffery asked.

"Yes, we actually have enough material on hand to build six of those structures."

"Okay. Oscar, tomorrow morning meet me at the shuttle port at eight o'clock and we'll go looking for locations to build your city. The shuttle holds twelve, so if you want to bring a few more people that would be fine. Have you given any thought to what you are going to call your city?"

54

"We haven't made a final decision yet, but so far everyone likes Procolt City."

"That sounds perfect," Jeffery said.

After everybody left Jeffery's office, except for Debbie, he asked her, "What do think about this?"

"I think it's a great idea, but we don't know anything about Oscar and his people. I think we should do some checking before we make any commitments."

"I agree. I'll compile a list of names and send it to Earth. We should get the information back in less than ten days.

The next morning Jeffery sent a message to one his contacts on Earth requesting information on Oscar and his group. Then Debbie, Mystic, and Jeffery went to the shuttle port. Oscar was waiting for them with two other people. When Jeffery was a few feet away he said, "Good morning Oscar. This is our daughter Mystic."

"Hello Mystic, my name is Oscar. And these are my friends, Trevor and Carol."

Mystic replied, "Hello, it's nice to meet you. My daddy said you want to move here and build a city."

"That's right. Today we're going to look for a good spot to build our city. You can help us."

Mystic smiled and said, "Okay, I think that will be fun."

Oscar said, "Trevor is an architect, and Carol is in charge of our finances."

Jeffery shook hands with Trevor and Carol. Then he opened the door to the shuttle and said, "Let's go."

After everyone was seated Jeffery announced, "The temperate area of Procolt 2 extends about four hundred units from the equator. Beyond that the winters are very severe, with temperatures below freezing for months at a time, so I think we should concentrate our search near the equator. Since you will need a source of water we should probably look for a location near a lake. All the lake water here is drinkable, although we filter it anyway.

"Lakes provide recreation too, Oscar said. Then he asked, "Are there fish in the lakes?"

"Yes, but we haven't found any that taste good. All the fish we serve comes from Earth."

"Part of the plan was to build a large fish hatchery," Carol said.

"I'm not sure that's a good idea. You mentioned you wanted to raise cattle and pigs yesterday. I was going to wait before I discussed the radiation here, but I think now is the time to tell you something about the environment of Procolt 2. As you know, the entire surface of the planet is bathed in radiation. It appears to have no effect on anything, except people and animals from Earth. It's beneficial, for the most part. Humans from Earth experience a substantial increase in muscle strength and extended life spans. Other species experience increased intelligence. I'm sure you are aware of the squirrels here. What you don't realize is that they are the result of mutated squirrels from Earth. If you bring animals here they may experience the same increase in intelligence. I don't think you would want to raise animals for meat that you could have a conversation with."

Oscar and his group were silent for a few moments. Then Oscar said, "That's an interesting development. I was wondering why there were no pets here. Now I know."

"Actually, there is no rule regarding pets; the situation has never come up. However, I don't think I would want the planet overrun with animals that are as intelligent as we are. If you want to raise animals for consumption you'll just have to import them from any planet other than Earth."

"With increased life spans, is this place the 'Fountain of Youth'? Do you have any information regarding lifespans for humans?"

56

"When we first arrived here we found the remains of a human who had been brought to this planet at the end of World War II. Tests indicated that he was about one hundred eighty years old when he died."

"Well, that would seem to be another excellent reason to move here."

"We have not made that information available to the public, and I'd like to keep it that way. Of course, none of us have been here long enough to validate the increased life spans for humans. However, on Earth squirrels live for about ten years. Many of the squirrels here are over thirty. By the way, the squirrels believe they are native to Procolt 2 and they are very proud of that. Please don't discuss this information with them."

"Of course not, nor will we discuss the increased life spans with other members of our group. If that information became public knowledge there would be billions of people here in a relatively short time."

"Exactly," Jeffery agreed.

The shuttle took off and Jeffery took them to a location a few hundred units east of Procolt Paradise. The area was surrounded by low mountains on three sides and there was a large lake in the valley. Jeffery guessed it was about twenty square units. Around the lake the land was mostly flat and filled with grass and trees. It looked like a perfect place to build a city.

"This was one of the locations we thought about for Procolt Paradise, but our lake is much larger. This lake is called Lake Meadows," Jeffery said.

"This looks perfect," Trevor said.

"I agree, I couldn't imagine a more idyllic place to build a city," Carol stated.

"Do you want to keep looking?" Jeffery asked.

"Can we land here and look around before I answer that question?" Oscar asked.

"Sure."

Jeffery landed the shuttle about two hundred feet from the lake. They all got out and began to look around. Everyone in Oscar's group was thrilled with the location. Mystic and Debbie went for a walk along the lake shore. The sky, which was clear, began to cloud up. It was almost time for the morning rain. As the first few drops fell they all went back to the shuttle.

Once they were inside Oscar asked, "What other places did you have in mind?"

"There is a location with a similar landscape three hundred units north of here. The biggest difference is the mountains are taller, and they are snowcapped. The temperature in the valley is cooler than it is here, and it does occasionally drop below freezing in the winter."

"Can you take us there?"

"Of course. I'll go slow so you can look at other areas. If you see something that looks interesting let me know."

"Thanks Jeffery."

Each member of Oscar's group was seated by a window. Jeffery kept the speed at about one hundred fifty units per hour so the trip would take two hours.

During the trip to the next location nobody found anything of particular interest. When they were almost there Jeffery said, "Look out the windows on the right side."

Almost in unison the three people in Oscar's group said, "Wow!"

Jeffery circled over the area for a while and then he landed the shuttle. The temperature outside was a brisk forty-two degrees. Jeffery handed each of them a jacket before they got off the shuttle.

Oscar said, "This place is really beautiful, but it's a little too cold to be comfortable. Is it always this cold?"

Debbie responded, "It is early winter here. In thirty days the high temperatures will hover around twenty-five degrees."

"How tall are those mountains?" Trevor asked.

"The air is very clear and it's difficult to judge distances by looking. The base of the mountains is twenty-five units north of our location. These are the tallest mountains on Procolt 2. They are all over one unit high, or in terms you are more familiar with, about six thousand five hundred feet," Jeffery said.

"Can you ski on the mountains?"

Jeffery shrugged his shoulders and said, "I don't know. I'm not into winter sports."

Oscar, with a note of authority in his voice, looked at Trevor and Carol and exclaimed, "As far as I'm concerned, the first location you showed us is perfect."

"I agree," Carol and Trevor said together.

"Good, let's go back to Procolt Paradise," Jeffery stated.

When they were back at the resort Jeffery suggested they meet at ten o'clock the next morning in the main restaurant. Everyone agreed.

Jeffery arrived at the restaurant a half hour early. An area at the back of the restaurant was set up where they would have some privacy during their meeting. He thought about holding the meeting in a conference room, but wanted it to be informal.

By ten o'clock everyone was there. Jeffery said, "Please sit down, relax, have some coffee and donuts. Jim, Oscar's group has chosen the valley around Lake Meadows for their city. How soon can you get started on their habitat?"

Jim thought for a few moments and said, "I can get started in two days. It will take three days to get the equipment and materials there to build it. When the outside of the building is finished I'll order the furniture, plumbing, kitchen fixtures, and other items needed to complete the job. The building will be ready for occupancy in thirty-five days."

Oscar smiled and said, "That's amazing. On Earth that project would probably take two years. There is a minor shortage of power modules on Earth now, so it would probably take a half year to get them. Where do you get yours?"

"Normally from Coplent. But we probably have at least five hundred in stock. If I order them my order always arrives in less than ten days. It's possible I'm getting special treatment, but I certainly never asked for it."

Oscar was obviously thinking about the timetable for the construction of the habitat. Then he asked, "I know we paid for more time here, but would it be possible for us to leave early and arrange to come back as soon as the habitat is ready?"

"If there is space available, I don't see any reason that couldn't be done. But the passenger ships are usually booked hundreds of days in advance. I believe you told me there are fifty-four people in your group. It may be difficult to accommodate that many people on short notice."

"Could you arrange for a charter ship to bring us to Earth and wait for us there until the habitat is ready and bring us back?"

"I'm sure I could do that, but it would be expensive."

"Please look into it. We plan on selling our property on Earth and that will give us the money we need to pay for the charter. If the ship is large enough I am sure we could have three hundred people from our group on the return flight."

"I will need five or six days to check for available ships. I'll send out a request today."

"Thank you. I don't think you realize how much this means to us."

"You're welcome."

Then Trevor asked, "Do you have any maps or images of the Lake Meadows area so we can plan our development?"

Jim responded, "Yes, we do. I would also like you to tell me where you would like the habitat to be constructed. Can you come to my office this afternoon at two o'clock?"

"We'll be there."

Jeffery sent out requests for a charter ship to Earth, Coplent, and Torblit. Every time he sent out messages he thought back to how easily things were accomplished on Earth and wished it possible to have instant communication again. But the distances involved made that unlikely to ever happen.

The following afternoon Jim met with Oscar and his group. Within an hour they had a preliminary plan for Procolt City and selected the construction site for the habitat. After the meeting ended Jim called his construction foreman and asked him to come to his office. When the foreman arrived Jim went over the plans with him and told him to start construction on the habitat as soon as possible.

Two days later the delivery of materials to the building site began. Although it wasn't required, a cement foundation was used as a base for the habitat. The building was less than a hundred feet from the Lake Meadows shoreline, and if the lake overflowed its banks he didn't want the habitat damaged. Most of the time the habitats are not intended to be used as permanent structures, but in this case it would probably be actively used for ten years or more.

The morning after the foundation was poured, Jeffery and Oscar were scheduled to go to the site to see how things were going. Before Jeffery went to meet Oscar, he stopped at his office to see if had received a reply concerning his request for information about Oscar and his group. The reply was there. Jeffery read it quickly and was relieved to see there was nothing derogatory in it.

Oscar was waiting for him when he arrived at the shuttle port. After they arrived at the construction site Oscar looked around and was very impressed. He said, "It would probably take a year on Earth to get this far, and your people have only been working on it for six days!"

"There's nothing to delay a building project here. No permits, environmental impact reports, or building inspections to contend with. If we want it, and have the material, we build it. By the way, I expect to get some response to my request for a charter ship today. We should stop by my office when we get back and check."

Oscar nodded his head in agreement. They spent another half hour wandering around the construction site and then returned to Procolt Paradise. They went directly to Jeffery's office, and as he expected, there were several responses to Oscars' request for a charter ship.

The most interesting response came from Greg Dorland. He was a space pilot who worked for NASA for twenty-five years. Greg found some financial backers, purchased a used ship, and spent a substantial amount of money refurbishing it. They took possession of the ship thirty days ago and were looking for their first charter. They were offering to do the charter for half of what the others were asking.

After looking over the bids Oscar asked, "Since you know people at NASA, could you check out Greg Dorland for me? The other bidders have all done charters before, but it's hard to ignore his price."

I agree. Actually, Brandon Simpson is on Procolt now, and he still works for NASA. Perhaps he can give us some information regarding Greg. I'll call him now."

When Brandon answered Jeffery said, "Hi Brandon, I have a question for you?"

"Okay, ask."

"Are you familiar with Greg Dorland?"

"Yes, I know him quite well. We have been on several missions together. He is an excellent pilot and engineer. Why?"

"He apparently has resigned from NASA and is now operating a charter business. I requested some bids on a charter from Procolt 2 to Earth and back again thirty days later for one of

62

our guests. Greg's bid was the lowest, by about fifty percent. But my guest is skeptical since he will be Greg's first customer."

"I wouldn't hesitate to book the charter with Greg. I would trust him with my life."

"That's exactly what you do if you book a charter. Your life is dependent on the ability of the captain of the ship."

"Yeah, tell your guest to go with Greg. I would."

"Okay, thanks Brandon. By the way, when are you leaving to conduct the Star Saver test?"

"At least another ten days."

"Okay, thanks Brandon."

Jeffery looked at Oscar and said, "Brandon knows Greg. He said Greg is an excellent pilot and engineer and he would trust Greg with his life."

"Okay, I guess we have selected our charter ship."

"I'll send him a message now telling him you agreed to his terms. When do you want him here?"

"As quickly as possible."

"Okay, I'll take care of it." Jeffery sent the message to Greg as soon as Oscar left the office.

Six days later Jeffery received a response from Greg that said he would be at Procolt the following day. Jeffery immediately informed Oscar. Oscar, and the other members of his group, spent the rest of the afternoon packing and planning for the return to Earth.

The next morning while Jeffery, Debbie, and Mystic were having breakfast in the main restaurant, a squirrel that Jeffery recognized walked up to their table. "Good morning Nathan, is there a problem?"

"No sir, everything is fine. But I was asked to find you and let you know that Greg Dorland would be landing on the next shuttle and he would like to meet with you."

Jeffery looked at his watch and realized the shuttle would be landing in less than ten minutes. "Contact the Captain of the shuttle and ask him to inform Mr. Dorland that I will be waiting for him here."

"Yes sir," and Nathan walked out of the restaurant.

"Who is Greg Dorland?" Debbie inquired.

"He's an ex NASA pilot who resigned and opened a charter company. He has a contract with Oscar's group to take them back to Earth and then return here when their habitat is ready."

"I'll bet when he sees you he calls you 'Admiral'."

"You're probably right."

Fifteen minutes later a man walked up to their table. He looked to be in his mid-forties. He was tall, and very muscular. He looked like a solider. When he was just a few feet from the table the man said, "Good morning Admiral Whitestone, good morning Captain Whitestone. I'm Greg Dorland. It's an honor to meet both of you."

"Thank you. It's a pleasure to meet you as well Greg. Please call me Jeffery and my wife Debbie. This is our daughter, Mystic. Please sit down and join us."

"Thank you, sir, uh, Jeffery."

"I was told you wanted to talk to me, but I have a question for you as well. Why did you resign from NASA? Brandon Simpson told me you were a top notch pilot and engineer. I'm sure you would have had an excellent future at NASA."

"I resigned from NASA because of you."

"What! You're going to have to explain that."

"You are responsible for the changes that have occurred at NASA over the past six or seven years. NASA is no longer a research organization. They are now a business entity, and one of the biggest on Earth. Their primary function is to build new ships and retrofit old ones. They also manufacture drive and communication systems for the entire trade group and are now the largest employer in the North American Union. And, as I stated before, these changes are your fault. You started them on the path."

"Okay, I see your point. The excitement is gone."

"Exactly. When was the last time you were on Earth?"

Jeffery looked at Debbie, hesitated for a few moments, and said, "It's probably close to nine years since we've been there."

"More than just NASA has changed. The native population on Earth has increased by thirty percent in the last four or five years, and there are now about a billion aliens living there too. Most of the major cities have outlawed private forms of motorized transportation. Inside the cities the number of single family homes has plummeted. The homes that were there have been torn down and replaced with high rise apartment buildings. New York, Los Angles, London, Tokyo, and Mexico City all have more than fifty million residents."

"Now I know why Oscar and his group want to move here."

"Oscar and his group are just the tip of the iceberg. There are groups like his all over the North American and European Unions. I'm sure you'll be hearing from them soon."

Everyone was silent for a while and then Greg continued speaking, "It's more than just the increases in population that are driving people away from Earth. The attitude of people has changed. Many of them have become lazy. The governments now provide 'cradle to grave' support for people who have no desire to work, and that number is growing every day. If you're happy with your life, why mess it up with work?"

"It seems to me that other civilizations in Earth's history have been in a similar position, and those civilizations withered and died. Is that what you think is going to happen on Earth?"

"Yeah, without innovation and exciting new products, Earth's finances will definitely take a turn for the worse. Someday somebody will invent a way to improve interstellar communications or develop a faster drive system and Earth will be left in the dust."

"They must realize that."

"You would think so, but I see no signs that anything will change in the future."

"They'll still have their food product exports, won't they?"

"Sure, but those exports only represent about eighteen percent of the total export revenues. About nine percent of our export revenues come from power module sales. However, our ability to manufacture products for our own use has fallen so far that there is now a six month wait for power modules. We manufacture them by the millions for export, but there is only one factory left that makes them for domestic use."

"So now the cities are overcrowded with people who are too lazy to work, and Earth no longer has the ability to meet its own energy requirements."

"Yup, that's pretty accurate. I think, or at least I hope, that eventually the people in charge will realize what's going on and take some action to reverse the situation."

"We are talking about politicians, aren't we? Until it affects them directly, they are unlikely to change things."

Greg sighed deeply and said, "I guess you're right. Anyway, how's the food here?"

"It's great, and it's free."

"That's a good combination. Do you know when Oscar and his group want to leave?"

"I suspect they will want to leave this afternoon. I told Oscar you would be here today."

"After breakfast I'll go find him."

Greg and Oscar's group left that afternoon. They were scheduled to return in twenty-seven days. The habitat was finished a few days ahead of schedule, so when Oscar returned, this time with two hundred thirty-three people, everything was ready for

66

them. Jeffery sent two shuttles to the space station to bring the new settlers directly to Procolt City.

The city grew rapidly. With the help of some of the construction people from Procolt Paradise, a half year later there were three more habitats built. One hundred nineteen farms, complete with homes, were ready to begin operation. There was a small shopping area too. Unlike Procolt Paradise, in Procolt City money was needed to buy things, so Jeffery had to begin producing currency. Something he knew nothing about, so he hired an experienced banker from Coplent to handle all the money issues.

By the time Procolt City celebrated its first anniversary, the population was twenty-seven hundred. Construction of farms was continuing and construction of some small factories were started. The first factory was going to make power modules. The second factory was going to make small electric vehicles for use in the city.

Procolt City continued to grow. As the fifth anniversary approached, the population was almost two hundred thousand. The city now had everything cities on Earth had. There were two hospitals and four shopping centers. The factories and farms were selling much of their output to Jeffery, but they were beginning to export things to other trade group members as well.

There was a big celebration for their fifth anniversary, and Jeffery was there with his family. Mystic, who was now almost fifteen, was there too, but she was not alone. She came with a boy named Stan. It was her first date.

During the ceremony Jeffery announced that he had been contacted by a group from the European Union that wanted to build a settlement as well. Construction on the new city would begin in about thirty days and was going to be named New Paris. Jeffery was worried the people from Procolt City might be concerned with competition from another city, but that wasn't the case. Oscar actually offered to help with construction.

During the five years since the first group of settlers came to Procolt 2, Greg Dorland's business grew as well. He now had five ships and the only charters they ran were between Earth and Procolt 2.

Crosus

About the same time the construction of New Paris began, Bejort Griss was finally about to receive the final version of the weapon he had been waiting for. It took almost three years longer than the engineers originally estimated, but he decided that by now his enemies would probably have forgotten about Crosus. But he was about to jar their memories. He summoned the commander of his armed forces.

When General Jastmore appeared at his office, Bejort found himself in an unexpectedly good mood. "General, please sit down."

"Thank you, sir."

"I'm sure you are aware that our new weapon is ready to be used to destroy our enemies. We will have three devices available in thirty days. I want you to arrange simultaneous attacks on Earth, Coplent, and Procolt."

The general smiled at Bejort and said simply, "No."

Bejort's mood changed instantly. He screamed, "What do you mean? Are you disobeying a direct order?"

"No sir, you are simply no longer in a position to give orders anymore. The planet in now under military control, and will remain that way until elections can be held."

"Are you out of your mind? I'm in charge here!" Bejort screamed.

Calmly the general said, "Screaming won't change anything. We have decided that we no longer have any desire to take revenge against those who were only protecting themselves from you and your inability to accept defeat. The other planets in the trade group where we were once a member are all flourishing, while our standard of living has fallen so far that in some parts of Crosus our people have almost no food."

Bejort looked at the general with hate in his eyes and said, "General, you are under arrest. You will not live to see tomorrow."

"Go ahead, call your guards."

Instead Bejort decided to take matters into his own hands. He opened a desk drawer, removed a weapon, pointed it at the general and said, "You're dead." Then he tried to fire the weapon. Nothing happened.

The general laughed and said, "Your weapon was disabled early this morning."

At that moment two guards walked in. The general said, "Please escort our former leader to the prisoner holding area in the Crosus Court Building."

One of the guards responded, "It will be our pleasure sir."

Once Bejort realized he was beaten, he surrendered completely.

Bejort's trial began two days later. He was charged with, among other things, more than five thousand counts of murder. He made no attempt to defend his actions and the trial ended quickly. Bejort was sentenced to death.

The day after his trial was finished, Bejort was taken to an old shuttle and was strapped into a seat. Next to him on the shuttle floor was the only completed weapon that had occupied almost his entire existence for the last eight years. Before the door to the shuttle was closed the general walked into the shuttle.

The general was smiling when he said, "You and your weapon, which has been disabled, will be able to spend your final moments together. After I close the hatch this shuttle will be sent on course directly to the sun. You have about two hours to live. I hope that perhaps you will spend your final moments thinking about all the misery you caused to the people of this planet, but I suspect you really have no remorse for the things you did."

General Jastmore left, closed the hatch, and moments later the shuttle departed. The general watched as the shuttle disappeared from view. Then he walked to his office, which was formerly Bejort's office, and sat down behind the big ornate desk. Prior to the coup he had arranged a meeting with the civilian leaders of Crosus for the next morning.

There were seventeen other people in the big conference room. General Jastmore stood up and said, "Today is a great day for Crosus. We are no longer controlled by a deranged leader whose only thought was revenge. However, I believe we have two tasks that must be completed as soon as possible in order to begin restoring our previous standard of living. The first is that we take whatever action is required to become members of the trade group again. I'm certain we will never regain our previous status with the group, but that doesn't matter. We need to be able to trade with other worlds to restore our finances. The second is that we must hold free elections. As soon as those elections are held I will step down and turn control of the government over to the elected civilian leaders. My assistant and I will be leaving for Earth later today. They are the most powerful member of the trade group now and we owe them an apology for our previous actions. We will be gone for about seventy days. I expect that while I'm gone the elections will be held. Is there anybody who disagrees with this plan?"

The other people in the room looked at each other, but nobody spoke. General Jastmore watched them and when he was sure there were no objections he said, "One more thing; while I'm gone I want all weapons research terminated. When I return we will consider filing criminal charges against some individuals involved in the development of the new weapon. In my absence General Yowlend will be in charge."

That afternoon General Jastmore and his assistant, Torpi Grwes, left for their mission to Earth. They were using a small unarmed ship they thought would not be considered a threat. It was equipped with the newest Crosus drive system, so it would take

71

less than thirty days to travel the one hundred light years to earth. During the trip, the General and Torpi spent most of their time rehearsing the upcoming discussions.

When their ship passed the orbit of Mars they contacted Earth's space station.

The General pressed the transmit key and said, "Earth station, I am General Jastmore from Crosus. I realize you don't allow ships from Crosus to dock at your location, but I'm hoping you will make an exception in this case. I would like to meet with a representative from the trade group to express our regrets for previous actions Crosus has been involved in, but the government on Crosus has changed and we want to rejoin the group."

A few moments later General Jastmore received a reply to his request. "General Jastmore, I don't have the authority to allow you to dock your ship here. Please hold your current position until I can discuss this with my superiors."

"Thank you, we will wait here. Please be advised that there are only two passengers onboard, myself and my assistant, Torpi Grwes. We, and the ship, are unarmed. You are welcome to inspect the ship if you desire."

"Please wait. I will contact the appropriate people immediately."

The general's ship was scanned several times. There were no weapons on board so none were found. However, the name Crosus is synonymous with death and deception. Several hours later the general received a call.

"General Jastmore, my name is Harlis Croter. I'm in charge of the trade group delegation on Earth. Your appearance here was something of a shock. We never expected any peace overtures from Crosus. I cannot permit your ship to dock at the space station at this time, but I can meet with you at our base on Mars."

"Thank you Mr. Croter, I appreciate this opportunity very much."

"I'll send you the coordinates of the Mars base. Meet me there in three standard hours. They will be expecting you. Please don't be offended when they search you for weapons."

"I understand the situation. We will not be offended by the search."

"Good, I'll meet you in three hours."

The Mars base consisted of six large interconnected transparent domes. There was one central dome and five domes around the perimeter. Each dome was connected to the central dome and each of the perimeter domes was connected to both of its neighbors. The domes were one unit in diameter and a half unit high. The base also extended about a half unit into ground under the central dome.

The general contacted the base and was given instructions on where to land. He landed the ship in the center of a large landing pad. As soon as he shut off the engines the pad began to sink into the ground. It continued to drop for a while and then it suddenly stopped. The general received a message telling him to move the ship forward, off the landing pad, and stop.

The general followed the instructions. As soon as the ship was off the pad it began its return to the surface. It appeared to rise much faster than it went down. Then the ship began to move forward. Ahead the general could see a pressure door. As the ship approached the door opened. Once the ship moved inside the door closed and the general could hear the sound of the area pressurizing. Then a vehicle appeared and stopped next to the hatch of the general's ship. He opened the hatch and four soldiers stepped inside. Two soldiers began inspecting the ship. A third man began checking the general and Torpi for weapons. When they were satisfied the fourth solider said, "Please follow me, Harlis Croter is waiting for you."

The general and Torpi followed the solider into the vehicle. A short time later the solider led the general and Torpi into a conference room. Inside three people were seated at the table. The man in the center stood up and said, "General Jastmore, I'm Harlis Croter. On my left is Krans Yondic. He's the local representative for the trade group bank. On my right is Colonel Halstead. He's in charge of the military contingent on Mars. Please tell us why you are here."

"I'm not sure where to start. Ten years ago it became apparent that Crosus was losing its position within the trade group. We needed money and discovered that Torblit had set up a mining operation on Procolt 4. The plan was to attack the mining operation and take the hirodim for ourselves. The Crosus leader hired some mercenaries to attack and kill the miners. The plan was that we would set up our own mining operation. It was thwarted by two people, one from Earth and one from Coplent. As a result of our murderous behavior, Crosus was expelled from the trade group. We have been suffering since that time."

The general paused for a moment and then continued, "The leader demanded we take revenge against both Earth and Coplent. He launched an attack to destroy Earth which failed, but killed more than ten thousand of Earth's people. He was not concerned about the deaths; he was only concerned that Earth survived and he lost again. He was overcome with rage and demanded our people build a weapon that would destroy Earth's sun. It took eight years to perfect the weapon. When I learned of his plan to use the weapon in simultaneous attacks on Earth, Coplent, and Procolt I arranged to take over the government and remove him from power. He is now residing on our sun for eternity."

"His lust for revenge almost bankrupted the planet. Many of our people are suffering from food shortages. Unemployment reached more than fifty percent. Without a change, we are doomed. I'm hoping you will consider allowing us to join the trade group again. We understand we owe reparations to both Earth and

74

Torblit, and when we have money again we will honor our obligations."

"We have idle factories and highly talented people who are anxious to return to work. Please allow us an opportunity to prove we can be a valuable part of the trade group again."

The three men looked at each other, all of them apparently surprised by the general's request. Then Krans Yondic said, "Prior to the expulsion of Crosus from the trade group, Crosus was our largest depositor. The funds in that account were frozen at that time. Since then we used the funds to pay reparations to Earth for the deaths and destruction of property caused by the attack. The families of the miners on Procolt 4 also received substantial payments from the account. Additionally, Coplent was reimbursed for the costs it incurred defending Earth. However, there is still more than two hundred thousand hirodim in the account. If Crosus becomes a member of the trade group again, those funds would be released."

The general smiled and said, "Thank you, I had assumed the money in our account was used to pay for our crimes, but I had no idea the remaining balance was so high. That money would allow us to buy things which are desperately needed."

Harlis Grwes said, "General, are you familiar with the name Hasin Tork?"

"Yes, he was in charge of weapons research. He disappeared several years ago."

"He didn't disappear. He defected and has been living on Procolt 2 with his family for several years. He assisted us in developing a system that would protect trade group planets from the device Crosus developed. That system has been deployed to protect most of the trade group planets. The attack your leader was planning would have failed again."

"I'm very happy to hear that, but even if I knew that our weapons would fail prior to the coup, it would not have changed anything."

Harlis Croter continued, "Will you agree to disband your military and allow the trade group to place military outposts on Crosus?"

"Certainly, that's a very reasonable request under the circumstances. I have directed the civilian leaders of the planet to hold elections in my absence. When I return I will step down and turn control over to the newly elected government."

"Does Crosus have substantial silver deposits?"

"I don't know, but I'm sure Torpi has the answer to that question."

Torpi said, "Yes, I do. Crosus has substantial silver deposits. Our manufacturing operation used more than one million golas of silver ever year. We don't use the same systems for weights, but one gola is slightly more than a half pound. Since manufacturing has declined by eighty percent after we were expelled from the trade group, silver mining has halted, but it would not be difficult to start it again."

"We have a problem here on Earth that Crosus may be able to assist us with. I'm sure you are familiar with the power modules we developed on Earth. We export them by the millions every year, and exports take priority over manufacturing them for our own use. As a result, we are experiencing shortages that are holding up major construction projects. Would you be interested in manufacturing them for us?"

"Yes, of course," the General replied.

"I'll have to discuss this with other trade group leaders. I'll need ten days to do that. I would like you to stay here while those discussions take place. Is that acceptable?"

"Yes."

"Good. We'll find a place for you to stay. You'll need visitor's badges to obtain the things you will need during your visit. We'll also give you communicators. Please feel free to explore the base here. A hundred thousand people consider this home. We have parks, restaurants, theaters, and a large sports complex. We don't use money on the base. That's why you'll need the badges. I'll make all the arrangements. Please wait here. I'll have somebody here to help you shortly."

The three men got up and left the room. After they were gone the general said, "That went much better than I expected. I was concerned we would be arrested and charged with war crimes."

"Bejort convinced us that the people from Earth were all evil and didn't deserve any of the benefits of being in the trade group. Obviously, it was all propaganda."

A short time later a young woman walked into the conference room. She said, "My name is Yolanda Grace. During your stay on Mars I'll be available to help you with anything you need." Then she handed the general and Torpi badges and small communication devices.

"If you need me press the green button on the communicator and say my name. The badges will be needed to obtain food or other items you need. Please follow me and I will show you to your apartments."

Yolanda, Torpi, and the general spent the rest of the day together. After she showed them their apartments she took them on a tour of the base. They ate lunch at one of the restaurants and it was the first time either the General Jastmore or Torpi had experienced Earth food. They were both very happy with their lunch.

After lunch she took them to one of the many parks on the base. This one had a small zoo and the General and Torpi were fascinated with the animals, which were completely different from the animals on Crosus. Then they went to the sports complex. Inside were areas for snow skiing, water skiing, swimming, golf, and tennis. Neither of the men from Crosus had even seen snow and they both decided to come back and try snow skiing before they went home.

By the time they returned to their respective apartments the General and Torpi were exhausted, and both went to bed early. For the next six days they explored the base and thoroughly enjoyed themselves. There was no place even remotely similar on Crosus. The general made a promise to himself that he would change that.

On the morning of their seventh day on the base General Jastmore's communicator beeped. He answered the call and Yolanda said, "Good morning General Jastmore. Harlis Croter asked me to bring you to the conference room at eleven this morning. I will be at your apartment at ten to bring you there."

"Thank you. Do you know what will be discussed at the meeting?"

"No, I was just asked to bring you there. I have no details at all."

"Okay, I'll expect you at ten."

Yolanda showed up right on time and found the general and Torpi waiting for her.

"Good morning gentlemen. Are you enjoying your stay here?"

"Yes," the general answered. "There is no place like this on Crosus. I can understand why so many people like living here. I've spoken with some of the people here and they all say it's much better than living on Earth."

"The big cities on Earth are overcrowded. There are lines everywhere. If you want to go to a restaurant for dinner you can usually expect to wait at least an hour for a table. If you want to go to one of the national parks you have to make reservations at least a year in advance, and if you want to stay at the park the usual wait is three years. Besides, many of the cities are located in areas where it's too hot in the summer and too cold in the winter. Here everyone has plenty of room, there are no lines for anything, and the temperature is always perfect."

"Can anyone just come here to live, or is there some process you have to follow?"

"In order to come here to live you have to have a job here. Every time we have any position available we get at least a hundred people applying for the job."

"What kind of jobs are there here?"

"This part of the base is all residential, but about ten units north of us are two more domes. There are factories inside those domes and we manufacturer a lot of things; primarily, small electronic devices and pharmaceuticals."

"How do the people get to their jobs?"

"There is a tram under the central dome. The tram runs between this area and the manufacturing area constantly. It's capable of moving fifteen thousand people per hour. The factories work on staggered shifts so the trams never become overcrowded." Then Yolanda glanced at her watch and said, "We have to go. We don't want to be late."

When they arrived at the conference room the same three men were waiting for them there. Harlis Croter said, "Good morning General Jastmore. I have discussed the Crosus situation with several of my colleagues and we are willing to give Crosus a chance to prove they can be a responsible member of the trade group again."

"Thank you. You really have no idea how much I appreciate this opportunity."

This time Krans Yondic, the military commander on Mars spoke. "General, the day after tomorrow a Coplent warship will be in orbit around Mars. Your ship will be placed in its hold and then you and your assistant will leave for Crosus. The trip will take four days. When you get there, you will turn control of your armed forces over to the commander of the Coplent ship. By the time you arrive the bank will have released ten thousand hirodim from your account. We want you to use that money to restart silver mining operations."

"That is all acceptable. Do you know what kind of facility will be needed to manufacture the power modules?"

Harlis responded, "No, but on board the ship will be two industrial engineers from Earth. They can give you the details of what is needed. I want you to assign somebody who is familiar with your manufacturing facilities to work with them. We are hoping that power module manufacturing can begin within one hundred days, with the first deliveries twenty days later. We will need at least five million units a year."

"Can we produce some for our own use?"

"Yes, as long as you meet your quota first."

"Will you guarantee us a specific profit margin? Obviously, we have to earn a profit on the devices we sell."

"We want you to keep accurate records of your costs for both labor and materials. We will pay you five times your cost on the first five million units. If additional units are needed we will discuss terms at that time."

"My only concern with any of this is that I will arrive at Crosus at least twenty-five days ahead of schedule. It's possible that the elections will not have occurred prior to my arrival."

"I'm sure you will be able to handle any domestic problems. I think you should arrange to speak to your people as quickly as possible."

"I agree, our previous leader had some supporters and I suspect they will not be happy with our arrangement, but I believe I can convince them that this arrangement is good for everyone."

Krans Yondic said, "I hope that it won't be necessary, but if military action is needed, your own military and the Coplent ship will be more than capable of handling the problem."

"I'm positive that won't be necessary, but it's always good to have options."

Harlis Croter said, "You and Torpi have another full day here. You should go enjoy yourselves."

"I think we will do exactly that."

Two days later they were on their way to Crosus. Shortly after the trip started, the general and Torpi were both in the general's cabin. They were discussing what they would do after they returned to Crosus. The door chime sounded and Torpi answered the door. There was a young female officer who asked, "I'm Lieutenant Kindler, are you General Jastmore?"

"No, I'm Torpi Grwes, his assistant. May I help you?"

"Yes, Captain Grotok asked me to bring you to the bridge. Would it be convenient for you to come now?"

The general walked up to the door and said, "Of course lieutenant, we would be honored to meet Captain Grotok."

The Coplent Warship was at least three times the size of the biggest ship in the Crosus fleet. It took almost a quarter of an hour to walk to the bridge. When they arrived Lieutenant Kindler led them to a door and knocked lightly.

A voice from inside said, "Enter."

The lieutenant opened the door and walked in followed by the general and Torpi. Once they were inside she said, "Captain this is General Jastmore and his assistant Torpi Grwes."

The Captain stood up, walked over, shook their hands, and said, "It's a pleasure to meet both of you. Please sit down."

The general and Torpi sat down. When they were seated it became obvious there were two more people in the room. The Captain said, "Gentlemen, I would like you to meet Luther Vandor and William Burtell, they are manufacturing engineers who will be

81

assisting you with the manufacturing facility needed to build the power modules."

The general said, "Gentlemen, it's nice to meet you. Please be assured that you will have our full cooperation in this endeavor."

William said, "Perhaps we can get together after dinner to discuss the requirements for the building."

"William, my assistant Torpi, is very familiar with the status of available manufacturing facilities on Crosus. I'm certain he can help you."

"Good, that's exactly what we need. Thank you general. We'll come to your cabin at eight if that's okay with you."

"Eight will be fine. Captain Grotok, I wanted to make you aware that Crosus has a substantial planetary defense system. It has a sensor range of more than three hundred thousand units. Please stop the ship at a distance of four hundred thousand units and I will contact them to let them know your ship is coming and not to take any hostile action."

"Thank you for the warning General Jastmore. I was going to ask you about that before we arrived anyway. I'll send somebody to bring you to the bridge at the appropriate time."

The two engineers arrived at the general's cabin right on time. Inside the cabin was a small round table and the four of them sat down. William Burtell began the conversation. "General, we want this endeavor to be a success as much as you do. The lack of power modules is beginning to have a negative effect on Earth's ability to provide housing for the constant flow of new immigrants. We need to build ten thousand homes every month to keep up with demand, but without an adequate source of power modules we are unable to meet demand."

"Why can't you use some of the units you are producing for export?" the general asked.

"Because the units used for export don't meet the power requirements we need for domestic use. I believe you know we have only one factory producing the units we need."

"Yes, Harlis Croter told me that during our first meeting."

"Anyway, what we need is a supply of pure silver, iron, and nickel. Those are the primary elements of the silver alloy rod that is the main component of the power modules."

"We have an abundance of those elements," Torpi said.

"The facility must have a high temperature furnace to melt the materials used to create the alloy and combine them with extreme precision. There is virtually no tolerance for error in mixing the components. After the alloy has been made it must be machined into rods. The size of the rod also must be exact. No dimension can be more than .0025 inches off. Do you know what an inch is?"

"Yes. After Earth joined the trade group their system of weights and measures was distributed to all the member planets. Since Crosus was still a member at that time we have the information," Torpi responded.

"I wasn't aware of that. Are you familiar with the basic concept of the design?"

"Yes. We managed to get some units and we took them apart trying to reverse engineer them, but we were never successful."

"The reason you were unsuccessful was because you didn't have the exact ratio of silver, iron, and nickel in the rod. If it's off by more than .02 grams the rod will be useless."

"That would make it almost impossible to analyze correctly."

"Exactly, that's the reason nobody has been able to duplicate the device. So, the power module is basically a transformer and the silver alloy rod acts as a magnetic amplifier. An unbelievably strong magnetic field is created when a small

83

electric current runs through the coil around the silver alloy rod. The positioning of the silver and iron rods is also critical. In power modules for use on Earth there is additional circuitry to convert the output of the transformer to a sine wave."

"Will you be supplying the circuit boards for the sine wave conversion?"

"No, you will have to build everything. We will supply you with the designs. Also, Luther and I will stay on Crosus until the factory is running. We will be able to provide any technical assistance you may need."

"I can think of several closed factories that have the facilities that will be needed. The best one is probably a factory that was used to produce various types of steel wire used in construction projects. It has the furnace we will need and it has assembly lines where the wire was wound on spools and packaged. I believe it could be converted in less than sixty days. We may not have everything we need, so we'll probably have to purchase some items from other trade group planets. That may be a problem."

Luther Vandor replied, "If there is something you need that is unavailable on Crosus, let me know and I will get it for you. We will not allow the fact that you are not a full member of the trade group stand in the way of this project."

"Thank you."

Then Luther, William, and Torpi spent two hours going over the power module design and the manufacturing process. It was way over the general's head, but he listened anyway.

When the meeting broke up and William and Luther left, Torpi said, "The situation on Earth must be critical. I'm grateful for that, because it works to our advantage. However, I can't help wondering why they just don't build another factory on Earth. There is something they're not telling us."

"I agree, but we must take advantage of the situation. I suspect we will eventually find out why they need us so badly."

The rest of the trip to Crosus went smoothly. They had a second meeting with Luther and William, but it was even more technical than the first one.

On the morning of the day they were scheduled to arrive, the General and Torpi were having a leisurely breakfast when Lieutenant Kindler appeared at their table. She said, "The ship will be stopping in .25 hours so that you can contact the Crosus security. Please come to the bridge with me."

When the General walked onto the bridge the Captain Gortek said, "Good morning General Jastmore. We will be stopping four hundred thousand units from Crosus in a few moments. There has been no evidence the ship has been scanned so they are probably not aware we are here."

When the ship stopped, Captain Gortek took the general to one of the communication consoles. The general set the transmission frequency and said, "Crosus planetary defense command, this is General Jastmore. Please respond."

A few moments later a voice responded, "What is the pass phrase?"

"Bejort has passed."

"Thank you general. You are not due back yet. However, I can see from this transmission that you're nearby."

"Yes, I'm a passenger on a Coplent warship. We will be parking at the space station shortly. My trip to Earth has been very successful and I would like to speak to the whole planet. Please arrange a press conference for us as soon as possible after our arrival and let General Yowlend know I have returned."

"Yes sir. I will take care of it. I'm very pleased your mission was a success."

"As am I."

An hour later the ship was parked. Captain Gortek, General Jastmore, and Torpi took one of the shuttles over to the space station. As soon as they stepped inside a group of at least thirty

85

people applauded. The general held up his hand and the applause stopped. One man, in military uniform, stepped through the crowd and walked over to General Jastmore. The man said, "General Jastmore, it is both an honor and a pleasure to meet you. I'm Commander Grimles. I've notified General Yowlend that you have returned and a representative from the government press office is waiting for you in my office."

"Thank you, commander. Have the elections been held yet?"

"No, the election is scheduled for ten days from today."

"Please lead the way to your office."

When they arrived at Commander Grimles' office they found that the waiting area had been converted into a studio of sorts. There was a desk at one end of the room, and a camera was mounted on a tripod a few feet in front of the desk. A man walked up to the general and said, "Sir, do you want me to ask you questions or do you just want to speak."

"I'll just speak."

The general sat down behind the desk. The lights in the room brightened and the man from the press office said, "Please speak now general."

"People of Crosus, I'm General Jastmore. I have just returned from a mission to Earth aboard a Coplent warship that is now parked at our space station. The purpose of the mission was to ask that Crosus be admitted to the trade group again. As you all know, we were expelled from the trade group for actions taken by our previous leader. To make the situation even worse, after our expulsion Bejort Griss almost bankrupted the planet in his attempt to take revenge against those he felt were responsible for our defeat."

"I have assured the trade group that we are no longer a threat to any other planet and want to rejoin the group so we can begin our recovery from the disastrous leadership of Bejort Griss."

86

"They have agreed to give us an opportunity to prove ourselves. We will immediately begin preparations to manufacturer a product for export to Earth. To manufacture this product, we will first have to reopen our shuttered silver mining operations and start retrofitting a factory to build the product. We expect the factory alone will employ at least five thousand people, and reopening the silver mines will get thousands of miners back to work. Our goal is to begin production within one hundred days."

"This is only the beginning. If we can attain full membership status in the trade group again, everyone will benefit."

"I have been asked to turn over control of our military to Captain Gortek, the Captain of the Coplent Warship, and I have agreed. After the elections I will turn control of the government over to the new leader."

"I hope all of you are as excited as I am about this change in our relationship with other planets. It will take time to rebuild and get our economy strong again, but I know we can do it. Thank you."

The reaction to the general's speech was overwhelmingly positive, although Bejort Griss still had supporters they were quickly silenced. The day after the speech a movement began to ask General Jastmore to run for leader. Five days before the election, the two civilian candidates who were running for the job contacted General Jastmore and asked him to run. They both said that if he agreed to run they would drop out. The general had no family so he discussed the situation with Torpi, who also thought he should run. Two days later the general reluctantly agreed.

When the election was held the general received ninety percent of the vote. After the election he resigned from the military, so now he was Leader Nalick Jastmore.

Two days after the election the first of the silver mines began operation again, after being closed for almost four years. Torpi, Luther, and William began touring potential sites for the factory that would build the power modules, and ultimately decided on the wire factory Torpi had originally suggested.

Work on refurbishing the factory began immediately. The old assembly lines were removed and the furnace was tested to make sure it was still functional. Luther and William worked for several days on the plans for the new assembly lines and gave Torpi a list of the things that would be needed. As it turned out, everything that was needed was either already available on Crosus or could be made within the required time. Nothing had to be imported.

They began hiring workers for the factory immediately. All would initially work on rebuilding the factory and then move into their permanent positions after the factory was operational.

While work was going on at the factory, three more silver mines were reopened and two facilities that produced pure silver bars from the extracted silver ore were reopened as well.

Luther and William were both impressed with the way things were going. It appeared they would have enough silver to build three hundred thousand power modules the day the factory began production. The required iron and nickel were brought to the factory site.

The circuit boards for the power modules were being built by a factory that was currently making electronic devices for domestic use, but they added another five hundred workers to build and test the power module boards.

Another factory was given the task of building the cases for the devices, and they too had to hire more workers to handle the task.

The effect on the Crosus economy was small, but for the first time in more than eight years it was moving in the right direction. Leader Jastmore received credit for the changes and in a poll taken a few days before the power module factory was scheduled to open more than ninety percent of the population was happy with the job he was doing.

The factory opened on schedule. During the first three days the factory was opened they produced fifty thousand silver alloy rods. That was enough to begin production of the power modules. To meet their quota they had to build almost seventeen thousand units per day. It took almost ten days to reach that daily requirement, but once it was reached it never faltered.

Every ten days a cargo ship from Earth would arrive to pick up the finished products. Within one hundred days the power module shortage on Earth began to disappear.

Crosus had proved itself and their membership in the trade group was restored. Almost immediately orders for products that Crosus had previously sold began to come in.

Additionally, now that Crosus was a full member of the trade group again, the new communication and propulsion systems were available to them. They sent ten of their cargo ships to Coplent to be refurbished.

Now that everything was running smoothly, Luther and William went to see Leader Jastmore to tell him they were returning to Earth. At the meeting Leader Jastmore asked the question that had been bothering him since their initial meeting on the Coplent warship, "Why didn't Earth simply build a new factory to make the power modules?"

Luther replied, "The people on Earth no longer want to work. Since the government has so much money they have become reliant on it for their needs. We could have built the factory, but it would have been almost impossible to find people to work there. Additionally, there is a silver shortage on Earth again."

Leader Jastmore said, "That situation, if it's allowed to continue, will have a substantial negative impact on Earth's economy."

"We know that. In fact, most of Earth's population realizes it. However, the people in a position to do something about the problem either don't know there is a problem or refuse to take any action they think might jeopardize their positions. Until the economy starts to falter and forces the people in authority to do something to correct the situation, there isn't much that can be done. Over the next year Crosus will probably be asked to manufacture more products for Earth. Can I assume you will be interested?"

"Yes, our economy is recovering, but it will take years before all the people who want to work will be able to find jobs again. I'm open to anything that will speed up the process."

"Thank you for your hospitality. It has been a real pleasure working with you and your people," Luther said.

"Thank you for your help. Without it I doubt we would have been able to accomplish the task that needed to be done."

For the next several years the economy on Crosus continued to improve. By the time Leader Jastmore had finished his five-year term as Leader of Crosus, it had become one of the main planets in the trade group again.

Procolt 2

While Crosus was rebuilding their economy, Procolt 2 was just beginning to develop theirs. There were now two large cities on Procolt 2. The larger one, Procolt City, had a population of almost a million residents. New Paris had a population of more than five hundred thousand people. The cities were booming and new residents arrived almost constantly.

Procolt 2 no longer relied on imports. Almost everything they needed, with the exception of some foods, was available from domestic sources. While the cities had grown so did the resort. It now had six guest towers, and tourists from almost every trade group planet had spent time there.

However, neither Jeffery nor Debbie were really happy with the situation. There was no real central government. By default, Jeffery was in charge, but he wanted that situation to end. Both Procolt City and New Paris had formed local governments, and each had a mayor. Jeffery contacted them and asked them to come to meeting.

There were only five people at the meeting. The two mayors, Jeffery, Debbie, and Mystic. Mystic was now almost eighteen and for the past several years she had been taking over more of the responsibility for running the resort. When everyone was seated Jeffery stood up and said, "Thank you for coming. As we all know the population of Procolt 2 will soon be two million people and we have no central government. Debbie and I have been doing the job, but it's not something that either of us wants to continue to do. I would like you two to work with us to form a planetary government, and when we are ready, we will have an election."

"In the near future we'll probably begin exporting some of our manufactured products. Thanks to the ingenuity of the squirrels, we have products that are not available anywhere else in

91

the trade group, and I'm certain there is a market for those items. We need to have our own currency and stop utilizing money from Earth. We need our own fleet of cargo and passenger ships. Additionally, at some point, we may want to curtail immigration. All these things, and more, are within the scope of a planetary government."

Mayor Haskell from Procolt City said, "I agree, Jeffery. We probably should have started on this a few years ago, but we were more concerned with local issues. I'm sure Mayor Cook feels the same way."

"I do. So far neither city has a crime problem, although we both have small police departments. Both cities have almost no unemployment and I'm sure that the availability of jobs is what is keeping crime to a minimum. However, as the population of our cities grow, we may soon find ourselves with some of the same problems they have in cities on Earth. The one I'm most concerned with is drug use. We must maintain zero tolerance for drugs. Unfortunately, what few drug problems we have had have been the result of tourists bringing drugs here. You have to end that."

"I know, and we are taking steps to do that now. About a hundred days ago we started scanning all luggage and people for drugs as they leave their passenger ships, but if we find anything we have no laws to prosecute them. All we can do is refuse entry to the planet. We have been giving them partial refunds, but that's going to stop."

Mayor Cook said, "That's a step in the right direction, but you're right, we need a planetary government. I suggest we take ten people from Procolt City, five from New Paris, and two from Procolt Paradise and give them the responsibility to draw up a constitution and some basic laws. Once that is finished we will have an election. I believe that anyone who lives here permanently has the right to vote, and I think that should include the squirrels."

"That sounds good to me," Jeffery said. "I think we should get started as soon as possible. As mayors of your cities you should be able to pick the people you need, but if you want to elect them, that's okay too."

"I'm sure I can find ten people for the committee," Mayor Haskell said.

"And I already have five people in mind. Jeffery, do you have any thoughts about your two members?"

"Yes, I was thinking about Mystic and Jessica Teacher."

"Those are interesting choices. I have no problem with either of them, but I'm curious about why you picked them."

Then Mystic said, "I'm curious as well Dad. Why do you want me on the committee?"

"Because I think Mayor Haskell and Mayor Cook are going to need leaders in their communities to represent their cities, which is perfectly logical. But I thought there should be some representation of our younger residents and the squirrels."

"Okay Dad, I guess that makes sense. But I don't think Jessica has the time to be a member of the committee."

"If that's the case I'll let her decide who should replace her. I would like the members of the committee to be finalized within ten days, and the first meeting scheduled as soon as possible after the committee members have been selected."

"I believe the North American Union has a constitution we can use as a start to build ours," Mayor Cook said.

"I'll get a copy of it and send it to both of you," Mystic responded.

"One thing I think you should consider. Instead of directly electing a president you may want to allow the government representatives we elect to pick somebody from their own ranks for the job."

"That would eliminate a lot of the problems I have seen with the governments on Earth. Sometimes it's impossible to

93

accomplish anything when the president and the congress have opposing points of view," Mayor Cook said.

Jeffery stood up and said, "At this point I'm removing myself from this situation. However, if you need my help with anything, please don't hesitate to ask. This meeting is adjourned."

After the meeting broke up Jeffery called Jessica and told her about the committee and that he had suggested she should be a member of it. She said she was honored that he thought about her, but she was way too busy to take on the additional responsibility. She also said she was pregnant and that would occupy some of her time as well. Jeffery offered his congratulations on her pregnancy and asked her to select another squirrel to take her place. She said she would get back to him in a day or two at the latest.

After the conversation was over, Jeffery began to think about the implications of Jessica's pregnancy. Since her child would inherit all of Jessica's knowledge and would learn more as it matured it would, in all likelihood, be the most intelligent being in the galaxy. He wondered what that would mean for Procolt 2.

Jessica did contact him and said she felt that her assistant, Timothy Baker, would be an excellent choice. Jeffery agreed and contacted the two mayors to let them know his selections had been finalized.

Two days later all the members of the committee had been selected and the first meeting was scheduled to begin at the Procolt City community center five days later and would last for ten days.

After six long meetings, the job was done. Copies of the Procolt 2 Constitution were distributed to all permanent residents and a vote was scheduled to ratify the constitution in thirty days.

The constitution was approved by ninety-three percent of the voters. Part of the constitution stated that there would be one representative in the Procolt 2 Congress for every hundred thousand people, except people who lived at Procolt Paradise would have two representatives. So, the first congress would have seventeen members. The same as the number of people who were on the committee to create the constitution.

The election was held thirty days after the constitution was approved. Most of the same people who were on the committee were also chosen for the congress, with one notable exception. Oscar Goodman was chosen as one of the representatives from Procolt City. At the first meeting of the congress, he was chosen as president.

As his first official act, President Goodman chose Mystic Whitestone to be his vice-president. It was an interesting choice. President Goodman was the oldest person in the congress and Mystic was the youngest.

The congress began work immediately. They created the Procolt Dollar as their currency, and set the value to be .0001 hirodim. This decision had to be approved by the trade group bank, and it was, but the bank required Jeffery to place one hundred thousand hirodim into an escrow account as a backup for the currency. That was not a problem. They also passed a one percent tax on all sales on Procolt 2 which was needed to fund the government. There were a few complaints about the tax, but in the end, it was accepted.

The decision was made to only pass laws that were needed to maintain the quality of life the people on Procolt 2 already enjoyed. They passed a law forbidding the distribution, use, or possession of drugs for recreational purposes. They also passed a law forbidding the development of new cities without the approval of the congress. The last thing they did before they adjourned was to create a police force and allocate the funds necessary to build two police stations, one in each city, and a small jail.

Until that time, personnel from Procolt Paradise manned the space station. Now that job was turned over to the police.

Jeffery and Debbie were sitting in Jeffery's office, each telling the other how happy they were with the way things were going. Jeffery said, "Now I'm able to devote all of my time to running the resort." But he admitted to himself that it was also a job he no longer desired.

"It is nice not to have to worry about a whole planet. I'm very proud of the job Mystic is doing as vice-president."

"I am too," Jeffery responded. He was about to say something else when Jessica walked into the office.

"Hello Jessica, how is your son Lance doing?" Debbie asked.

"He's doing great. I expect him to begin speaking in another ten days or so. Anyway, I have something exciting I want to discuss with you."

"Okay, what is it?" Jeffery asked.

"Currently small electronic devices like communicators and hand-held computers use batteries. Battery technology has not exactly kept pace with other scientific advances, although most devices only require a battery change annually. My team and I have developed a new battery, based on cold fusion technology, which will last forever."

"That is exciting!" Jeffery exclaimed. "What would be involved in producing them?"

"First, we have to finish our testing, but so far we have not encountered any problems. The batteries are fairly simple to make, but they will be expensive to manufacture in small quantities. However, I estimate that once we are making a few million of them per year, the cost will drop to about three Procolt Dollars each."

"How long before the testing is complete?"

"Probably less than a hundred days."

"Can you build some samples for me?"

"Of course. I need to know the size, voltage requirement, and how many you need."

"I would like the type that fit into communicators. I think I'll need at least fifty of them."

"I can do that. I'll have them for you in five or six days. What are you going to do with them?"

"I want to take them to Earth and sell them. Since Earth manufactures almost all the communicators used in the trade group, it would seem like the best place to start. In the meantime, I'll contact one of the industrial engineers in Procolt City and have him come here. I would like you to meet with him and discuss the manufacturing requirements."

"Okay, I must tell you that this is the most exciting thing I've done since I worked on the communication and propulsion systems."

"Thank you for doing this. These batteries are going to do wonders for the Procolt 2 economy, which was doing well already."

"You're welcome."

After Jessica left Debbie said, "You know I'm going to Earth with you."

"I wouldn't dream of going without you. It's been years since we've gone back to Earth. I know it's changed a lot since our last visit, and not for the better, but I want to see it for myself."

The next day Jeffery sent a message to Terrance Brennan, the Director of Operations at NASA, telling him that he and Debbie were coming to Earth for a visit and they would be there in fifteen days. They were planning on staying on Earth for two weeks and he wanted to meet with him during that time.

He also sent a message to Kimberly Thompson, the Director of Research and Development at Apex Electronics. Apex Electronics supplied more than seventy percent of the hand-held communicators used on the trade group planets. He had met Kimberly before at a conference that was held several years previously on Coplent. He told her he had something that he was positive she would be interested in and asked her to set up a meeting while he was on Earth.

97

Six days later he received responses from both of the people he contacted. Both of them gave him several choices for dates and times. He selected a date and time for both meetings and sent that information back to confirm them.

The next day a squirrel delivered fifty sample communicator batteries to his office. He called Jessica, thanked her, and then told her he was leaving for Earth the following day.

Earth

Jeffery arrived at the space station three days later. He contacted them, identified himself, and asked for a parking location.

The man Jeffery was speaking to on the space station was so surprised he was almost unable to speak. He stuttered when he said, "Admiral Whitestone…It is an honor to speak with you sir…I was told you were coming. Please bring your ship to shuttle bay seven. You can park your ship inside the station."

Jeffery said, "Thank you." Then he moved his ship to shuttle bay seven. As he approached the exterior door opened and he flew his ship inside and landed. The exterior door closed and he could hear the shuttle bay pressurizing. An alarm sounded when the pressurization was completed. When he heard the alarm, Jeffery opened his ship's hatch. He grabbed the suitcase they had brought and followed Debbie off the ship.

Seconds later the door to the interior of the space station opened and a man wearing a uniform Jeffery did not recognize walked up to him and Debbie. He extended his hand toward Jeffery and said, "Hello sir, it is a pleasure to meet you and Captain Whitestone. I'm Captain Kingsley, the manager of the station. Please follow me. There is a shuttle waiting to take you to NASA headquarters.

Jeffery shook his hand and said, "Thank you, Captain. I was not expecting this kind of greeting. Neither of us are in NASA anymore."

"We know that sir, but both of you are still celebrities on Earth."

Captain Kingsley led them to a shuttle bay a few hundred feet away and opened the door for them. Inside was a small shuttle. Jeffery and Debbie walked inside, and Captain Kingsley followed them. He smiled and said, "I'm also your pilot for today. Please make yourselves comfortable. The trip will take about an hour and a half."

Debbie said, "Thank you, Captain Kingsley."

"Things have changed since your last visit. The area around NASA headquarters is now filled with tall buildings. All of them are a combination of apartments, offices, and stores. For many NASA employees, there is no reason to ever leave their building."

"Is that a good thing?" Debbie asked.

"Well, to be honest, it's not the lifestyle I would choose, but for some it's perfect."

The shuttle landed and Captain Kingsley said, "We didn't announce your arrival at headquarters so you won't be mobbed. I was told to take you directly to Director Brennan's office."

"We have a meeting scheduled with him in five days. Why would he want to meet with us today?" Jeffery asked.

"He didn't tell me anything other than to bring you to his office as soon as you arrive. You'll have to discuss the other meeting with him."

As they stepped off the shuttle there was an open tram waiting to take them to the headquarters building. The tram ride was short, less than a mile.

They entered the building and stopped at the security desk. There were badges already waiting for Jeffery and Debbie. The man at the security desk said, "Good morning Admiral Whitestone," as he handed Jeffery his badge. Then he said, "Good morning Captain Whitestone," and gave Debbie her badge.

Noting the rank of the man at the security desk Jeffery said, "Thank you, Corporal."

Captain Kingsley said, "I won't be attending the meeting. However, I will be waiting for you here. I'll have a car here in a few minutes and I can take you wherever you want to go."

"Thank you. We'll be staying at Brandon Simpson's home while we are here. Is that okay?"

100

"Of course, I was there once for a party. It's a beautiful place."

"Yes, it is. Although it's been a long time since we've been there, I'm sure it hasn't changed very much."

Jeffery and Debbie got into the elevator and took it to the top floor. When they stepped off the elevator a young woman was waiting for them. She said, "Director Brennan is waiting for you. Please follow me."

They followed the woman to a large, and rather ornate, wood door. She opened it, and then moved to the side so Jeffery and Debbie could enter the office. Jeffery scanned the office. It was enormous, at least fifty feet long and thirty feet wide. The walls were covered with a beautiful dark wood paneling, and on the walls were pictures commemorating the greatest moments in NASA history. Included were several pictures of Jeffery taken during his years as a pilot. There were also pictures of Debbie, and three pictures taken during their wedding.

A tall, broad shouldered man got up from behind the desk at the far end of the room. He walked over to them and as he approached he said, "It's a pleasure and an honor to meet both of you. As you can see from the pictures, you two were a very important part of our history. Please allow me to introduce myself; I'm Terry Brennan. But call me Terry. If it is okay with you I'll use your first names as well."

"Actually, we prefer it, Terry. Debbie and I never liked titles."

"Please sit down. Would you like something to drink?"

"Yes, a real cup of coffee would be very nice," Debbie said.

Terry picked up his phone and a moment later said, "Please bring in coffee for us." Then he looked at Jeffery and said, "I know we have a meeting scheduled for five days from now. That's an official meeting, this one isn't. May I ask what brings you to Earth again? I believe it's been eight years since your last visit."

101

"The length of time since our last visit is one of the reasons for this one. I'm sure you are aware that more than one and a half million people have immigrated to Procolt 2 in the last five years. The stories they have told me about life on Earth doesn't match my memories. I want to see it for myself. Debbie feels the same way."

"There is no doubt that Earth has changed, and many of those changes can be traced back to you two. Because of you, Earth has experienced a level of economic prosperity we had never experienced before. That's the good part. However, the governments were unable to contain themselves. They spent the money they had, and a substantial amount they didn't have. They were positive the good times would last forever. Wages and benefits increased all over the planet. Then the governments decided to raise the standard of living for everybody. They began paying people who didn't work almost as much as the people that did. As a result, it became difficult to find workers for factories, so a lot of those jobs were replaced with machines. That meant many of the people who were working became unemployed, but it didn't really matter because they were getting paid anyway. However, it did matter to the governments. With fewer people working, tax revenues plummeted. None of them are bankrupt yet, but it could happen."

"So, because of a lack of workers Earth had to outsource a lot of their manufacturing to Crosus?"

"Yes, exactly. As you probably know NASA is now the largest employer in the trade group. We have more than eight hundred thousand employees. We build new ships on Earth, Coplent, and Torblit and we have large maintenance facilities where we maintain and retrofit ships on Earth and Coplent. Almost all of this work has to be done by people; it can't be done by a machine. We pay well, more than twice what you would get from the government for not working, and that's a starting salary. It goes up from there."

102

"It sounds like you should have people banging on your doors looking for jobs."

"You would think so, but we don't. We currently have more than two thousand job openings at this facility. During a good week we might find twenty people who actually want to work."

"Wow! Earth is a victim of its own success," Debbie said.

"Yes, we are. We have been forced to import workers from other planets, which is adding to an overcrowding problem in the major cities all over the world. While you are here you should go spend some time in New York or Mexico City. You will probably think you're on Coplent, not Earth. By the way, the European Union is now considering a ban on extraterrestrial workers."

"That will probably make a bad situation worse."

"Yeah, I'm sure it will. Anyway, you said there were two reasons why you are here. What's the other one?"

Jeffery reached into his pocket and retrieved one of the sample batteries. He handed it to Terry and said, "This is the other reason."

"It's a battery. Is there something special about it?"

"Yes, it's a cold fusion battery that will last forever. It was developed by my research and development group."

"You mean the squirrels, don't you?"

"Yes, they surprised me with this about twenty days ago. I had no idea they were even working on it."

"Do you expect it to replace the power modules?"

"No, it's a low power device. It's designed specifically to be used in low voltage and low current applications, like communicators and hand-held computers."

"You'll be able to sell these by the millions. Where are you going to manufacturer them?"

"We're going to build a factory on Procolt 2. Tomorrow we have a meeting with Kimberley Thompson of Apex Electronics. I'm sure she will be interested."

103

"Yes, I agree. Tell me, do you have a willing work force on Procolt 2?"

"Yes, our unemployment rate is about one percent. There are no welfare benefits on Procolt 2. However, we've formed a government now so that may happen in the future. The people who came to Procolt 2 to live want to work and be productive. They weren't looking for handouts. These people built their own cities. They built homes, stores, farms, and factories. I provided some of the money, but they did the work."

"Would you be interested in having a NASA facility on Procolt 2?"

"I'll certainly think about it. How big would it be?"

"There would be a space station used for large ship assembly and a factory complex where small ships and parts are manufactured. I would guess it would require about ten thousand employees."

"That's an interesting proposition. We don't have ten thousand unemployed people, but I'm sure we could get people from Earth to move there. I'll discuss it with you at our next meeting."

"Be prepared to be mobbed by reporters at the next meeting."

"Okay, I'm not worried about it. I've handled reporters before."

"Jeffery and Debbie, once again, I want you to know it was very nice finally meeting you both. I'll contact you the morning of the meeting and arrange to have somebody pick you up."

"Thank you, Terry. Debbie and I have a lot of thinking to do before our next meeting."

As promised, Captain Kingsley was waiting for them in the security lobby. Jeffery and Debbie returned their badges and followed the Captain to the car. It was a big car, probably twice the size of any car they had on Procolt 2. Once they were comfortably seated Jeffery asked, "Captain, why is somebody with your rank driving us around?"

"I volunteered for the job, but I have an ulterior motive. I want to discuss something with you in private."

"Okay, I can't imagine anything more private than a car. What did you want to talk about?"

"I have advanced degrees in electrical engineering and physics, but on Earth we don't do much research and development anymore, and that's what I want to do. I would like to work on Procolt 2 in your research labs."

"Do you realize that the research and development on Procolt 2 is done primarily by squirrels?"

"Yes, I know that. But that doesn't bother me. I know how intelligent they are and that demands respect. Their physical appearance means nothing. I have seen some videos of S12 speaking and she was very impressive."

"I have something I want to show you when we stop."

"Because of traffic it will probably take at least an hour to get there. Would you like to stop somewhere for lunch?"

"I'll leave that to you. The rest of our day is free."

"Okay, I know the perfect place."

They drove for a while before the Captain stopped the car in front of a restaurant called, Mark's Old Fashioned Diner. He said, "This place has terrific food. I'm sure you will like it. All the meat here is real, not made from vegetable protein like most of the meat that's served on Earth now. That stuff may be healthier, but it tastes like crap as far as I'm concerned."

"On Procolt 2 we import beef, pork, and chicken from Earth and Coplent. It's all very good," Jeffery responded.

"I thought there were farms on Procolt 2. Doesn't anybody raise animals for consumption?"

"No, there are no animals raised for food on the planet."

"That's strange. Why not?'

"It's something I'm not prepared to discuss at this time."

The Captain looked like he was going ask something else but finally said, "Okay."

The restaurant was crowded and they had to wait for a table. That was something Jeffery and Debbie had not experienced for a long time. After they were seated and ordered their lunch, Jeffery reached into his pocket and took out a sample battery. He handed it to Captain Kingsley and said, "This is our latest development. It's a cold fusion battery that will last forever."

The Captain took the battery, looked at it for a while, and said, "This is exactly the kind of project I would love to work on."

"If you're sure you want to move to Procolt 2, send a message to Jessica Teacher, she was S12 when she was visiting Earth, and tell her you want to join her group and why. Include all your qualifications and what you think you could add to the group. If she says she wants you, it's a done deal."

"I'll do that this evening. Thank you."

"If you join her group you will be the second human in it. Brandon Simpson is also in the group. Have you met him?"

"A few times when he passes through the space station, but we've never really talked other than the normal pleasantries. Because he usually uses his own ship he doesn't come to the station very often."

When they arrived at Brandon's house Bess and Tom were waiting for them. Jeffery introduced Captain Kingsley. There were a few hugs and Bess said, "Your room is ready, and if you tell me what you want for dinner I'll make it."

Debbie responded, "We're not that particular. Make whatever you want. I'm sure it will be fine."

"Okay, I hope you like peanut butter and jelly."

Debbie laughed and said, "If that's what you want to make that's okay with us. I don't think I've had a peanut butter and jelly sandwich for twenty-five years."

106

"I'll surprise you with something for dinner, and it probably won't have peanut butter in it."

"I have to get back, but if you need me to drive you someplace just let me know," the Captain said.

"Thanks for the offer, but Brandon has several cars here we can use if needed, although neither of us has a valid driver's license anymore."

"That's not an issue. They stopped requiring driver's licenses several years ago. The only requirement now is you must be over sixteen. Since all the cars have collision prevention devices there are very few accidents. Most cars can also be driven by the onboard computer, so everything is automatic. I prefer to drive myself, but most people like the automatic driving capability."

"Perhaps we'll see you again when we go back for our next meeting with Terry."

"Probably not, I'll be on the space station. Please let me know as soon as you hear from Jessica."

"I promise."

When Jeffery and Debbie were alone Jeffery asked, "Do you like the idea of having a NASA facility on Procolt 2?"

"I've been thinking about it since Terry mentioned the possibility. I think it's probably a good idea. It helps make us more independent."

"Ten thousand new jobs probably means another fifty thousand people on the planet. I know that's not a problem now, but I think now is the time to start thinking about controlling immigration."

"That's not your problem anymore. You gave up control, and now you have to live with that decision."

"I know, and I think it was the right decision to make. But I still can have opinions, can't I?"

"I suppose."

The meeting with Kimberley Thompson was set up for the following morning at Brandon's house. Kimberly arrived a few minutes early and Bess brought her to a table by the indoor pool where Jeffery and Debbie were waiting.

Jeffery stood up as Kimberly approached and said, "Good morning Kimberly, it's nice to see you again. This is my wife, Debbie."

Kimberly reached forward, shook hands with Debbie and said, "It's a pleasure to meet you, Debbie. Jeffery said a lot of very nice things about you when we were together at a conference in Coplent a few years ago."

"I was planning on going to that conference with him, but our daughter was sick and I didn't want to leave her. Anyway, it's nice to meet you as well. Please sit down."

Jeffery and Kimberly both sat and Kimberly said, "You promised me something that I would be interested in, so what is it?"

Jeffery picked up a small open box that was on the floor and put it on the table in from of Kimberly. She removed an item from it, looked at it, and said, "It's a communicator battery, I have a hundred thousand just like it in stock."

"No, you don't. I guarantee you don't have any like these batteries."

"Really? What's so special about these batteries?"

"They'll last forever. They use cold fusion technology. Unless they are physically damaged, they will continue to produce power indefinitely."

Kimberly smiled and said, "That is interesting, but what do they cost?"

"That depends on how many you buy, but it'll be a small fraction of what you'll be able to charge for them. I promise you, I won't sell them directly to your communicator customers."

"I assume these are for me to use for evaluation purposes?"

"Yes, those are for you."

"Where are they going to be manufactured?"

"I recently decided that since Procolt 2 has a permanent population approaching two million people, any new products we develop will be manufactured on Procolt 2."

"That's a wise position to take. I heard Procolt 2 now has a government. Is that true?"

"Yes, and my daughter Mystic was selected to be vice-president."

"Congratulations, how old is she?"

"Almost eighteen."

"That seems very young to have that much responsibility. Will she be able to handle it?"

"Yes, she's been running Procolt Paradise for over a year, and we have over ten thousand employees. Debbie and I are not involved on a daily basis. About the only thing we do is greet visitors as they arrive."

"I'm sure if she can run your resort successfully she is qualified to be vice-president. Usually vice-presidents don't do very much, but it's good experience if she wants to make a career in politics."

"I think she wants to continue running the resort. I would guess she's not really interested in politics. Anyway, to get back to our discussion of the batteries; assuming you find the samples acceptable, how many do you think you would need going forward?"

"We sell about a hundred thousand units per month, and I would guess 90% of those sales would include your battery. I would also expect to sell an equal amount of batteries to existing users. So, for the first few years about two and a half million units per year."

Jeffery said, "Okay, I'll get back to you with a cost estimate in ten days or so. That will give you time to evaluate the samples.

I would suspect that battery sales to existing users would drop after a few years as units in the field are fitted with the new ones."

"You're probably right, but if Apex is the only company selling communicators with these batteries, our market share will probably grow and new unit sales would increase. How soon can you begin manufacturing?"

"About one hundred fifty days after we receive a signed contract."

"I have one more question; is there any danger of a radiation leak if the batteries are physically damaged?"

"No, the reaction generates almost no radiation, and the battery components are minimally radioactive. Industrial antistatic devices are more radioactive than battery components are. I also have a question for you. How does Apex find workers to build the products you manufacture?"

"We don't look for workers, we build them. We even have robots to maintain the robots on the production line. It's almost impossible to find workers on Earth now. The factory that builds the communicators only has nine employees. Their primary job is to program the robots that build the communicators."

Kimberly left a little while later and Jeffery immediately sent a message to Jessica with production requirements. He also told her that she would be receiving a resume from Captain Kingsley. Jeffery realized he didn't know Captain Kingsley's first name and made a mental note to ask him the next time they meet, which would probably be before their next meeting with Terry.

At dinner that evening Debbie asked, "We said we were going to stay on Earth for ten days. I want to spend two days with my parents and sister. We haven't seen them since they came to the resort last year. What do you want to do with the rest of our time here?"

"I want to spend a day or two with my parents too. After our meeting with Terry, I think we should go to New York, San

Francisco, and Paris. We're isolated here. I want to see if things in the big cities are as bad as we've been told. We may have to extend our stay by a day or two."

"I like your idea. Two days in each location should be sufficient for us to see what's going on."

"I'll make all the arrangements this afternoon. We'll go see your mother first."

"Let me call her before you make any reservations. I want to find out what her plans are."

"Okay, when we know their schedule I'll call my father."

Debbie went to Brandon's office to call her mother. She sent her a message before they left Procolt 2, so her mother was expecting the call. It was a long conversation. Her mother started the conversation by complaining about living in a big city. After listening to her diatribe for a while Debbie asked, "Would you like to live on Procolt 2? There are no crowds, no lines, you can use your own car to get around, and we'll get to see each other all the time."

"I was hoping you would ask me that question, so I wouldn't have to ask you. We're ready to go tomorrow. Your sister wants to move there too. Would it be okay if we came down to Florida to see you instead of you coming here?"

"Sure, we're staying at Brandon Simpson's house. It's really beautiful. I'll make the arrangements and call you back."

"That isn't necessary. Your father and I can pay for our own tickets. We can even afford to buy Connie a ticket too."

"I'm sure you can, but Jeffery and I are probably the wealthiest people in the trade group. We have more money than we can ever spend, so please let me take care of the tickets. When do you want to move?"

"I wasn't kidding when I said we're ready to go tomorrow. If there is room on your ship, we would be happy to go with you when you go home."

"Will Connie be ready to leave immediately too?"

"I'm sure she will be, but I'll ask her."

"Should I just buy one way tickets?"

"I'll call you back in a half hour."

"Okay, I won't do anything until I hear from you."

Debbie went back by the pool area to tell Jeffery about the conversation. She sat down at the table and said, "There's been a change in our plans. My parents and Connie are coming here tomorrow."

"That's not a problem. There's plenty of room here. We just have to let Bess know so she can get two more guest rooms set up."

"There's more. They don't want to go back home again. They want to move to Procolt 2 and want to go back with us."

"I think that would be okay. Do they want to live at Procolt Paradise or one of the cities?"

"I don't know. We can discuss that with them tomorrow. They would have to stay at the resort until we can get a house built for them anyway."

"Are they going to let us have a house built for them? Your father is a very proud man."

"I'm not sure. I just had to convince my mother to let me pay for the tickets to Orlando."

"Perhaps tomorrow we can discuss the financial part of this move. They own property here. Are they going to sell it?"

"Good question. I have no idea. Anyway, you should call your Mom and Dad. Do you think they want to move too?"

"I actually offered to build them a house in Procolt City if they want to move. My Dad said he would think about it, and we haven't discussed it since then."

"You should tell them my parents are moving. Perhaps that would help them reach a decision."

"I'll mention it to him."

Jeffery left the pool area, and like Debbie, went to the office to call his parents. They knew he was on Earth because he sent them a message the previous evening. When he called his father answered the phone.

"Hello Jeffery, we have been waiting for your call."

"I've been tied up in meetings since I got here, and this was really the first opportunity I've had to call you. How are you and Mom doing?"

"We're doing great! When we heard the news that Mystic is now vice-president we were so proud of her. I wish we could see her more often."

"You can. We discussed this last year. Debbie and I would really like to have you and Mom living on Procolt 2. Debbie's parents are going home with us and they're going to stay there."

"I discussed this with your mother before. She said she has friends and obligations here, but I'll ask her again. Debbie's mother and father live in one of the cities, don't they?"

"Yeah, and they don't like what's happened. That's why they want to move. I realize you live in a rural area and don't have the same problems, but Procolt 2 is a much nicer place to live."

"I agree, I'll talk to her tonight at dinner. Are we going to see you and Debbie while you're here?"

"Of course, I'll call you tomorrow and let you know when we'll be there."

"Can you call me in the morning around ten o'clock? I'll make sure your mother is here."

"That's no problem. I'll call you tomorrow at ten."

He walked back to the pool area and saw Bess. He told her Debbie's parents and sister were coming tomorrow and would be staying for a while, and asked her to prepare two guest rooms for them.

Bess said she liked having more guests and was happy to make up the rooms.

113

When Jeffery got back to the pool area he sat across the table from Debbie and said, "I spoke with my Dad. I'm sure he wants to move, but he's not sure how my mother feels about it. He's going to talk to her tonight and I'm going to call him back at ten tomorrow morning."

"While you were talking your Dad, Connie called me. She said she wants to move immediately too. So, it looks like we'll have three passengers on the return trip.

The next morning Jeffery called his parent's house and his mother answered.

"Hi Mom, how are you?"

"I'm fine. Your father and I had an interesting conversation last night about moving to Procolt 2."

"And did you come to a decision?"

"There's something you don't know. Your father has some health issues. He's developing one of the few diseases that we haven't found a cure for; Parkinson's. I'm sure he didn't tell you that."

"No, he neglected to mention it. But you should know we have doctors, hospitals, and all the latest medical equipment on Procolt 2. I doubt there's anything that can be done to help him on Earth that we can't duplicate."

"I think you missed the point I was trying to make. He's sure he doesn't have very long to live, and wants to finish his life on Procolt 2. Despite the fact I will be leaving lifelong friends, he comes first. So, I agreed to move. But, we are going to need some help."

"I'll get you all the help you need."

"We have to sell our house and all our household items first, don't we?"

"No, you don't have to sell anything. I'll take care of all your expenses. You can either stay at the resort or I'll have a house built for you. It's your choice. We'll put the house up for sale after you move."

"Are there really good doctors there? I'm worried about him."

"I know Mom. Yes, we have two excellent doctors on staff at the resort, and I have access to the best medical care in the trade group if that becomes necessary."

"Okay, I know medical care can be expensive, but I also know that you and Debbie are very wealthy. Will his expenses be a problem?"

"No Mom, I'm sure I can afford whatever medical help Dad needs. Please don't concern yourself with money."

"Thank you. Are you coming here to see us?"

"Debbie's parents and sister are coming here today. We're going to spend two days with them and then we'll come and see you and Dad. We'll be there the day after tomorrow, probably in the afternoon."

"It will be nice to see you again."

"After you move we can see each other as often as you like, especially if you are living at the resort."

"Your father is out walking. I'll let him know about our conversation when I see him. Please don't mention his medical problems unless he brings them up first."

"Okay, I'll see you in a couple of days. Bye."

"Goodbye Jeffery."

Jeffery found Debbie sitting in the living room listening to music. It wasn't something she did frequently, but she was obviously relaxing and enjoying it. She didn't even notice when he walked into the room. But when he tapped her lightly on her shoulder she looked up at him, smiled, and asked, "What's the verdict?"

"They're moving. My Dad has Parkinson's and is convinced he's going to die soon, and he wants to spend the end of his life on Procolt 2 with us. So, my mother agreed to move."

"People don't die from Parkinson's anymore, do they?"

"Not on Procolt 2. In severe cases, the disease can be debilitating, but it's no longer terminal. Anyway, we have to go and pick up our guests. Their flight will be arriving in less than two hours. Tom picked out a car for us to use."

"Is it fully automatic, or will you have to drive?"

"Do you trust me to drive?"

"No, not really."

"I don't trust myself either. The car is totally automatic. All we have to do is tell it where we want to go."

They got into the car. Jeffery was sitting in the driver's seat. He pushed the start button and a voice asked, "Destination please?"

"Orlando airport."

"Arrival or departure?"

"Arrival."

"Airline and flight number?"

"North American Air Express, flight number 1684."

"That flight is currently on schedule to arrive at two o'clock. We will be there fifteen minutes earlier."

The car began its journey. Neither of them had ever ridden in a self-driving car before, and they both found it somewhat disconcerting. After about ten minutes they realized there was no reason for concern, so they started talking about their parents.

When the car stopped the voice said, "We have arrived at our destination. The flight has been delayed by five minutes. Please take a remote from the compartment in front of you and push the button when you are ready to be picked up. When the light turns green it means I will be here in three minutes."

Jeffery opened the compartment and took one of the small remotes. Debbie took one too. They got out of the car and walked inside the terminal. A large monitor hanging from the ceiling had flight information displayed on it. The flight they were waiting for had landed, but would not be at the gate for another fourteen minutes.

They sat down in the gate area and waited for the flight. While they were waiting, a security officer walked up to them. He said, "Are you Jeffery and Debbie Whitestone?"

"Yes, is there some problem officer?"

"Not really. But for security reasons we don't allow famous people to wander around the airport unescorted. So, if you don't object, I will be staying with you until you leave."

"How did you know we were here?"

"Your car informed us."

"That's interesting, the car making sure we're safe," Debbie said with some amusement in her voice.

"Please join us officer."

"Thank you, sir, may I ask why you're here?"

"My parents and sister are arriving on flight 1684," Debbie answered.

"I know a lot of people have left Earth and moved to Procolt 2. It's in the news all the time. Is Procolt 2 that much nicer than Earth?"

Jeffery said, "Why don't you come and see for yourself?"

"On what I get paid? My wife and I would have to go for ten years without eating to be able to afford that kind of vacation."

"I think I can take care of that. Give me your name and address and I'll arrange for a free thirty day vacation for your family. Do you have any children?"

"No sir, it's just my wife and me."

"The vacation is for six, so if you want to invite anybody else just include them on the reservation form. All I need is your name and communication number."

The security officer stammered when he said, "Thank you sir, nobody has ever done anything like this for me before. I can't tell you how much I appreciate it." Then he handed Jeffery a card and said, "This is my contact information."

Jeffery took the card, glanced at it, and said, "Your welcome, Officer Jensen. Somebody from reservations will call you in about seven days." Then Jeffery handed him one of his cards and said, "If you haven't heard from them in ten days call me and I will take care of it personally."

At this point the officer was speechless, so he just nodded in agreement.

When the plane reached the gate, Debbie's parents and sister were among the first to disembark. There were hugs and kisses and then Jeffery asked, "How much luggage do you have?"

"We each brought two suitcases. We figured that anything we didn't bring we could buy," Debbie's father responded.

"Okay, let's go get your luggage."

By the time they arrived at the baggage claim area their bags were waiting for them. Officer Jensen brought over a luggage cart and put the bags on it. Then he said, "I've already called your car, it should be waiting by the time we get to the curb."

The car was waiting for them. Officer Jensen put the bags in the trunk. Then he turned to Jeffery and said, "Thank you again sir. May I contact you again when we are at Procolt Paradise?"

"Of course. Thank you for your help with the luggage."

"You're welcome."

After everyone was in the car Debbie looked at Jeffery and said, "You just gave that guy a three hundred thousand dollar tip!"

Jeffery smiled and said, "It was the least I could do since he was risking his life to protect us."

They spent the time in the car talking about things that had happened in the past year. Nobody discussed the move to Procolt 2.

When they arrived at Brandon's house, Bess and Tom were there to greet their guests. Jeffery introduced everyone and Bess showed them to their rooms. Then she gave them a tour of the property.

While Bess was giving them a tour, Jeffery received a call from Captain Kingsley who told him he would be there at nine o'clock to pick them up for their meeting with Terry. That evening at dinner Jeffery told Debbie's parents and Connie that he and Debbie had a meeting the next morning with the director of operations at NASA. They expected to be gone most of the day.

Connie said, "I could easily spend a month here. I think we can survive for a day without you guys."

"Yes, I'm sure of that. If you need anything, just ask Bess."

Captain Kingsley arrived right on time. After they were seated Jeffery asked, "What's your first name? I don't want to call you 'Captain' all the time."

"It's Vince. This is supposed to be a secret, but there will be somebody else at your meeting with Director Brennan this morning. Gerald Wilson will be there as well."

"That was unexpected. Why would the president of the North American Union want to meet with us?"

"They don't tell me anything. I found out only because I saw his shuttle land this morning at seven o'clock. I checked the security roster for the day and saw that he was scheduled to meet with Director Brennan at eleven. Can I assume you haven't heard from Jessica yet?"

"Yes, the earliest I would expect a response is tomorrow. I'll call you as soon as I get her message."

Vince dropped them off at the NASA Headquarters Building and said, "I'll be back in an hour and the meeting is scheduled for two."

Debbie and Jeffery walked into the building. The same security guard was on duty. He said, "Good morning," and handed them their badges.

When they got off the elevator the same woman greeted them and took them to Terry's office. She knocked, opened the door, and moved aside so Jeffery and Debbie could step into the room.

Seated at a conference table was Terry and President Wilson. They both stood up. Jeffery and Debbie walked over to the table and Jeffery said, "Good morning Mr. President. This is an unexpected pleasure."

President Wilson shook hands with Jeffery and Debbie and said, "Good morning. It's nice to meet two people who I have read so much about over the years. Are you really surprised to see me here?"

"No, the man who drove us saw your shuttle this morning and saw this meeting on the security logs. But it's still a pleasure to meet you."

They all sat and President Wilson said, "The reason I'm here is because I want to discuss something with you."

Jeffery nodded and President Wilson continued, "I'm sure you are aware we have labor problems on Earth. There is an extreme shortage of factory workers. It's beginning to undermine our ability to remain competitive within the trade group. I know this is a problem we created, but neither me, nor any of my advisors, have any suggestions to resolve the problem. I was hoping that perhaps an outside viewpoint might be helpful."

"I was made aware of how serious this problem is only a few days ago, and I have been thinking about it. I think the only thing you can do is cut the fluff out of payments to those who don't want to work because they are very comfortable. You have to make them uncomfortable enough so they will want to return to work."

"That's a perfect recipe for losing the next election."

"First, I think if you are honest with the people they will respect your decision. They may not like it, but as long as they realize the need for it, the majority of the people will continue to support you. Even if you lose the next election, you still have the satisfaction of knowing that you did the right thing."

"What do you think Terry?"

"I agree with Jeffery, I don't see another solution. We can't continue to outsource our manufacturing and retain our standard of living. We either have to reduce our standard of living for everybody, or just for those who don't want to work. You should know that because of a labor shortage I asked Jeffery if we could build manufacturing and repair facilities on Procolt 2."

"Did you agree?" President Wilson asked.

"I haven't given him my answer yet, but Debbie and I have discussed this and believe it's a good idea. Even though I'm not a part of the Procolt 2 government, I will do everything I can to make us self-sufficient. Five years ago, before Procolt City was fully functional, we imported everything. Now we make about eighty percent of what we need. Most of the remaining twenty percent are food items we can't produce on Procolt 2."

Terry asked, "I thought you were importing cars from Earth?"

"We were until sixty days ago. We are still taking delivery of cars purchased prior to that time, but there will be no new orders. Our factory in New Paris is now making about three hundred cars a day, and we could increase that by adding additional workers. If we were running the factory around the clock we could make over a thousand cars per day."

"Do you use all manual labor?"

"No, some repetitive tasks are done by machines, but eighty-five percent of the manufacturing utilizes manual labor."

"Are all the parts made on Procolt 2?"

"Yes, we don't have to import anything."

121

"That's amazing. I'm sure at some point we could have done the same thing on Earth, but it would be impossible now," President Wilson said.

Nobody said anything for perhaps thirty seconds, then President Wilson said, "Jeffery, the measures you are suggesting are not something I can do on my own. It requires Congress to pass new laws. Would you be willing to speak to a joint session of Congress and tell them what you just told me?"

"Why me? I'm not a great public speaker. I'm positive you could present the same information much more eloquently than I could."

"People think of me as a politician. You, however, are considered a hero by most people of the world. They believe all the good things that have happened on Earth over the last ten years are because of you and Debbie, and they are right. You made contact with the people from Coplent, you played an important role in our joining the trade group, and finally the technology developed on Procolt 2 is the primary factor in Earth's phenomenal economic growth."

"So, you're saying you think they will take action if I tell them something, but if you said the same thing it will just be political claptrap."

"Yes, that's exactly what I'm saying. Will you do it?"

"Okay, but I need a few days to prepare something. Do you have a speech writer I can work with?"

"Of course, I'll have Brenda Murray contact you tomorrow. She helps me with most of my speeches.

"Debbie and I were planning on going home in ten days or so, but I guess we can stay a little longer."

Debbie, who had not said a word during the conversation, said, "This is very important and delaying our return by a few days isn't a problem. I know you don't like speaking to large groups, but you've done it before and did it very well. I'm sure you'll do just fine."

"Okay, I'll call a joint session of congress in ten days. That will give you plenty of time to prepare."

The meeting broke up a short time later. Vince was waiting for them in the lobby of the building. Jeffery told Vince what happened at the meeting and the three of them spent the entire trip back to Brandon's house discussing what Jeffery should say in his speech.

As they pulled up to the house Jeffery said, "Vince, I should have received a message from Jessica this morning. Do you want to come in?"

"Of course; I'm very anxious to hear from her."

They went directly to Brandon's office. Jeffery checked his messages and there was one from Jessica. He told Vince about the message and then opened it. The message said, "I'm sure you wouldn't have asked Captain Kingsley to contact me if you didn't feel he was qualified to work here. His credentials are excellent. So, as long as you feel he would be an asset to our work, I'm all for it."

"The job is yours. Call me whenever you're ready to go."

"Thank you, sir. I'll have to give NASA a thirty day notice that I am leaving. I'll send that in tomorrow."

The following day Jeffery and Debbie spent the morning working on Jeffery's speech. In the afternoon Brenda Murray called. Jeffery told her the speech was mostly completed and she asked him to send it to her. He did that as soon as their conversation ended.

The next morning Jeffery received a message from Brenda. Attached to the message was the finished speech. Jeffery read it and thought it was very good. He gave it to Debbie; she liked it.

Jeffery and Debbie decided to postpone their trips to the big cities. They spent two days with Debbie's family and then they went to visit Jeffery's parents. After greeting each other they sat on sofas in the living room and Jeffery's father said, "We've talked it over and decided we would like to move to Procolt 2. We appreciate your offer to buy us a house, but we would prefer to live at Procolt Paradise. Is that possible?"

"Of course, Dad," Jeffery responded. "You can have one of the high-rise apartments or a house. It's your choice. Regardless of the one you choose, you will get daily maid service, all your meals are free, and you can use any of the resort's facilities."

"We will need thirty days or so to do some things before we leave. Can you arrange for transportation?"

"That won't be necessary. Debbie and I aren't very busy anymore, so whenever you're ready send me a message and we'll come back and pick you up. We'll be here three days later."

"Thank you."

"You're welcome."

Jeffery and Debbie spent two days with his parents before returning to Florida. After they returned Jeffery's mood changed. It was obvious he was concerned about the speech and that concern intensified as the big day approached. He practiced the speech every day, and now he remembered the whole thing.

Vince contacted him the day before the speech to tell him he would be there to pick them up at six thirty in the morning. The speech was scheduled for one o'clock.

The morning of the speech Jeffery's mood was better. He realized he was not a politician, and if he didn't deliver the speech perfectly it really didn't matter. His life was on Procolt 2, not Earth.

There was a NASA shuttle waiting for them when they arrived at the shuttle port. The flight to Washington was smooth and relaxing. He and Debbie talked about their parents and other things, but neither of them said a word about the speech.

A limo met them at the shuttle port in Washington. When Jeffery and Debbie stepped off the shuttle, Beth Kessler, the vice president, was there to greet them. They shook hands and got into the limo. They went directly to the chamber where the event was to be held. Then Ms. Kessler took them to a room where there was coffee and snacks. Jeffery and Debbie each had a cup of coffee. They sat there until five minutes before one. Ms. Kessler stood up and said, "it's time to go."

She took Jeffery to the staging area, and directed one of her staff to take Debbie to her seat. At precisely one o'clock the Sargent-At-Arms announced Beth Kessler. She walked up to the podium and spent several minutes speaking about Jeffery's past. Finally, she introduced him and Jeffery walked up to the podium. They shook hands again and Jeffery said, "Thank you, Madam Vice-President, for that wonderful introduction. I don't remember doing all the things you mentioned, but my memory probably isn't as good as it used to be."

There was some laughter and applause. When it quieted down Jeffery began speaking. "Thank you all for coming today. I have never spoken to a group like this before, but the message I have for you transcends my discomfort with the situation. Earth is in trouble. Like many of the great civilizations of the past, Earth is about to become a victim of its own success. It happened to the Greeks and the Romans. I can only hope it won't happen again."

"The financial success of the last ten years has brought unprecedented wealth to the governments of Earth. It's natural for governments to distribute some of that wealth to the people they govern. They are elected by the people to their positions and feel compelled to give something back. That's not a problem when it is done in the form of tax breaks, free education, and health care. Responsible governments also provide assistance for those that are unable to take care of themselves. However, it becomes a problem

125

when governments provide direct financial assistance to those people who simply don't want to work."

"The average unemployment rate in Earth's largest metropolitan areas is at an astounding nineteen percent. It's not because jobs are unavailable, it's because the people who receive payments from the government collect only slightly less than what they would be paid if they worked. In their minds, they can easily forgo some material items in exchange for not having to get up and go to work every day."

"Because it's no longer possible to find workers for Earth's factories, many of those products are now being manufactured on other planets. Earth alone is responsible for the financial resurgence on Crosus."

"I would like to tell you about a situation I discovered shortly after I arrived on Earth. I had a meeting with the director of operations at NASA. He told me that at any given time NASA has at least a hundred jobs available at their location in Florida. Many of these jobs do not require advanced education or special skills, they only require a desire to work. NASA will provide the training required for the job. These positions go unfilled because during a typical week only five people apply for jobs."

"On my home planet, Procolt 2, we did not have a government until recently. There was no welfare and everybody worked. Now that we have a government, I hope they will pass whatever laws are needed to provide assistance to those who truly need it. But I'm positive they will never pass a law that provides financial assistance to people who don't want to work and expect the government to take care of them. However, laws like that would never be considered since the people who came to Procolt 2 did so because they saw what was happening on Earth and wanted to escape before the governments here collapsed. These people built their own homes, stores, and offices. They started farms to provide their own food. They built the roads, shuttle ports, and bridges. In short, they built their own cities."

"That attitude still exists among many of the people on Earth, but it is up to you to rekindle the spirit of your citizens. To do that you will need to pass some unpopular legislation. You must reduce the payments to those who are unwilling to work to a point where it makes them uncomfortable. Millions of people will be upset with you if you do this, and you may lose the next election, but you will save the Earth for future generations. Thank you."

Most of the people in the audience applauded. Others sat in their seats and were obviously upset with Jeffery's comments.

The following day the media and some of the more influential members of congress reacted to Jeffery's speech. The conservatives felt the speech was to the point and accurately outlined the problem. The more liberal members of congress and the media were actually offended by his comments. Jeffery really didn't care what anybody thought. He did what President Wilson had asked, and now it was up to President Wilson and others in government to resolve the problem.

The day after the speech Jeffery, Debbie, and her family all left Earth for the trip to Procolt 2. Vince called Jeffery that morning to tell him that he had given his thirty-day notice to NASA, and he would be available to start work on Procolt 2 immediately after that. Jeffery said he was coming back to Earth in thirty days anyway to pick up his parents and bring them to Procolt 2 and Vince could join them.

During their trip back to Procolt 2, legislation was introduced in the congress of all seven of Earth's governments. President Wilson and other conservatives were more than a little disappointed that Jeffery's speech was not as well received as they had hoped. President Wilson's economic advisors told him that without the legislation the government would have to begin borrowing money again to pay the benefits required under the current laws. He also knew what would happen if the legislation was passed by the North American Union, but not the other governments: The people who were happy being dependent on the government for their existence would move to other parts of the world. That would not be a bad thing for North America, but it could be devastating for the other groups. He decided that was not something he was going to worry about.

Jeffery's ship landed at Procolt Paradise. Mystic was there to greet them. She didn't realize her grandparents and aunt were coming, so she was pleasantly surprised to see them. Jeffery said, "Your grandparents and Connie are staying here permanently. Please find them nice two bedroom apartments."

"Okay, Dad. Several apartments were just vacated on the sixty-third floor overlooking the lake and the marina. I'm sure they'll like them. Come on, I'll show them to you."

Debbie's mother said, "I know it's been a while since we've been here, but you have really grown up. Your Dad said you are running the resort now and you are also Vice President. That seems like a lot of responsibility for somebody your age."

"I guess you're right, but I don't think about it very much. It all just seems to come naturally."

Debbie's parents and Connie went with Mystic to look at the apartments. Jeffery walked over to the lab to speak with Jessica.

When he walked into the lab Jessica looked up from what she was doing and asked, "How was Earth?"

"It's changed a lot, and not for the better. I'll tell you about it later. I want to let you know that Apex expects to buy two and half million units per year initially, so we need to begin working on both the manufacturing facility and the process to make them in large quantities."

"Would it surprise you if I said I was already working on that?"

"No, it wouldn't surprise me at all."

"I would like to use squirrels to build the batteries. They are better suited to work with the very small components in the batteries."

"That's not a problem. All the squirrels are excellent workers. Where do you want to build the factory?"

"I would like to build it near Procolt Paradise, in the meadow about a unit north of here."

"Okay, the resort won't expand in that direction anyway. When can you have the design complete so Jim can start construction?"

"Probably twenty days from now. Some of the heavy equipment will have to be ordered from Earth, but I'll get that ordered in a few days."

"Do you think we could be in production in a hundred days?"

"Probably, but give us an extra twenty days just in case we find an unexpected problem."

"Okay, I'll send a message to Kimberley at Apex and let her know. She's going to ask about the cost, so I'll need a price in six or seven days."

"Actually, I should have that for you by tomorrow."

"Thanks Jessica, as usual, you are doing a wonderful job. I'm going back to Earth in thirty days to pick up my parents who are moving here. Debbie's parents and sister are here permanently too. They came back from Earth with us. Anyway, when I return Vince Kingsley will be with me, so you might want to think about his first assignment."

"Okay, I'll think about it."

The following day Jeffery received a call from Jessica who told him the manufacturing costs for the batteries, in Earth dollars, would be $2.17 each. Jeffery thanked her for the information and immediately sent a message to Kimberley telling her the cost for the batteries, based on annual purchase of two and a half million units was $12.17 per battery. The profit from the sale of the batteries would easily pay for the manufacturing facility.

Jeffery received a message from Kimberley six days later agreeing to the terms. She said the samples were excellent, and was sure she would be able to sell them for $35. Obviously, everybody was going to make a profit on this product.

Jeffery and Debbie went back to Earth on schedule, picked up his parents and Vince, and returned immediately to Procolt 2. When they landed Mystic was there to greet her grandparents. She had already selected an apartment for them, so after an affectionate greeting, she took them to their apartment.

Jeffery, Debbie, and Vince went to Jessica's lab. Jeffery made the appropriate introductions and then he and Debbie went to the restaurant to get something to eat. Jessica gave Vince a brief orientation, showed him to his apartment, and took him on a tour of Procolt Paradise.

While Jeffery and Debbie were eating, Jim came over to their table and told them that construction had started on the battery factory. He expected it to be operational in less than one hundred twenty days.

When Jeffery returned to his office there was a message from Terry telling him he would be coming to Procolt 2 in thirty days to discuss the NASA facility he wanted to build. Jeffery realized now that Procolt 2 had a government, he had to inform them about his discussions regarding the NASA facility. He called Mystic and asked her to come to his office.

Mystic walked in and said, "Hi Dad. What's up?"

"You need to put on your Vice-President hat for this. When I was on Earth the first time, NASA asked me about the possibility of building a facility here that would build and repair ships. Before I left I agreed, but I neglected to inform you or Oscar. Anyway,

Terry Brennan will be here in thirty days to discuss the details and somebody from the government needs to be involved."

"I have a meeting with Oscar tomorrow morning. I'll discuss this with him then. I assume they want to build here because they can't find employees on Earth."

"You're exactly right."

"I can't imagine Oscar objecting, but I'll let you know what he says after our meeting."

"Thanks."

"You're welcome, Dad."

During the next year and a half several things happened. The battery factory was finished and was producing more than ten thousand batteries every day. Construction had begun on the NASA facilities. The new NASA space station was only about half completed, but the ground facility had opened for business ahead of schedule. Business at Procolt Paradise grew at an almost alarming rate, so two more guest towers were built and ready to open. Both towers were already fully booked for a year.

Everything on Procolt 2 was going well. The new government appeared to be functioning well, and Mystic was doing a great job as vice-president. Unfortunately, Earth was experiencing some serious issues.

Earth

A year and a half after Jeffery's speech, things on Earth had gotten worse with the exception of North America and Asia. They passed laws to limit the payments of those who simply refused to work. President Wilson's prediction that the people who expected the government to support them would move to other locations where that policy was still in effect, proved to be correct.

The influx on new residents in Europe and Africa forced the governments there to raise income taxes and they added other taxes that hit the middle and upper classes the hardest. As a result, the productive people left these areas and moved to either North America or Asia.

Now the European Union and the African Union were facing bankruptcy. Both had debts they would never be able to repay, so they turned to North America and Asia for financial help. Although the money was available to bail them out, both North America and Asia refused unless the laws were changed to eliminate the problem.

After the refusal, the European and African unions decided to cut back services and eliminate government jobs in order to attempt to balance their budgets. It was a dismal failure. Finally, in an act of desperation, the people of Europe elected new government leaders. New laws were passed and the European economy began a slow recovery. The unemployment rate dropped to under ten percent for the first time in more than ten years, and as unemployment dropped, tax revenues increased. It appeared Europe was on its way to becoming solvent again.

When the Africans saw the European recovery they also began to implement the same policies. A year later Africa was on the road to recovery as well.

Earth 2284

Terrance Mason was elected to the Presidency of the North American Union in November, 2284. The economic problems Earth had suffered through ended more than twenty years earlier. Earth was going through another economic boom, unemployment was at one percent, the population stabilized at twenty-two billion people, and life expectancy on Earth had reached a new high at one hundred ten.

President Mason was in the third month of his term. Yesterday, one of his scientific advisors, Dr. Richard Grant, called and asked for a meeting to discuss an urgent situation. The president asked him for details, but Dr. Grant said it was best to explain the situation in person. The meeting was scheduled for ten o'clock, and Dr. Grant was right on time. The president's secretary opened the door to his office and escorted Dr. Grant to a chair across the desk from President Mason.

After the secretary left the room the President said, "Good morning Richard. What's the urgent problem?"

"The entire western half of the North American Union could be destroyed in a cataclysmic volcanic eruption in two years! I believe that should be considered urgent," Richard responded.

"If you're correct that is certainly an urgent situation. Please explain what you think is going to happen."

"I'm sure you know we are now able to predict Earthquakes with ninety percent accuracy within a thirty day period. The accuracy drops to fifty percent at a year. Four months ago a team from the University of Montana predicted a 2.7 magnitude Earthquake in the Yellowstone Basin within sixty days. There was a quake fifty-eight days later that registered 2.8 on the Richter Scale. After that quake, they predicted another one in forty days that would register 3.1. That quake occurred two days ago. Since the first 2.8 quake there have been hundreds of smaller

133

quakes occurring every day, but those quakes are slowly increasing in strength. Since then there have been nineteen quakes that were over 2.0, and five of those were over 2.5. Yellowstone National Park is sitting on one of the largest volcanically active areas in the world. I believe a major eruption will occur there within two years. If my calculations are correct, the eruption will occur in conjunction with a 9.8 quake. The strongest Earthquake ever recorded was 9.5; this quake will be significantly larger. I think the area between Juneau and San Diego will be demolished."

"More than a billion people live in that area! What can we do?" the president asked anxiously.

"I believe that the only way to stop the quake is find a way to release the pressure building up under the Earth's crust, but I have no idea how to do that. I have spoken to a few engineers I know and asked them if there was any way to release the pressure that is being generated by a pool of lava. They all basically said it was impossible."

President Mason was silent for a few seconds and then he said, "I thought earthquakes only occur on fault lines, where tectonic plates meet."

"Your right, most earthquakes are along the edges of tectonic plates. However, earthquakes directly beneath a volcano are caused by the movement of magma. The magma exerts pressure on the rocks above the magma and eventually they crack resulting in a quake."

"Maybe we just need better engineers?"

"Yes, I agree. I want to go to Procolt 2 and discuss this with the squirrels."

"Okay, I'll send a message to Jeffery telling him that we need his help."

I thought his daughter, Mystic, was running the place now. I know she took a vacation from running the resort while she was president of Procolt 2, but that was almost thirty years ago."

"She has been running the resort since that time with her husband, a man from Procolt City named Virgil Griffith. They have a son named William who is now about fifteen years old. Anyway, Jeffery is still involved in research projects, despite the fact that he is now over a hundred years old. He was here for my inauguration and looked like he was in his forties. Take the ship that leaves on Friday. That way Jeffery will have some time to prepare for your arrival. I'll let him know why we need him as well."

"Thank you, sir. One more thing; I think you should consider closing Yellowstone and Grand Teton. If the predictions are correct, the next powerful quake will occur in about sixty days, and that quake will be about 4.2. That's enough to damage roads, bridges, and masonry buildings."

"I don't want to scare people. Let's try to get some answers first."

"Okay, sir. I understand. I'll get you the information as quickly as possible."

Procolt 2

Jeffery sat down at his desk and checked his messages. He was surprised to see an urgent message from Terrance Mason. He met Terrance when he came to Procolt Paradise for vacation twenty years ago, and he and Terrance had been friends ever since. The three-day travel time between Earth and Procolt 2 meant they didn't see each other very often, but they sent messages to each other frequently. This was the first time he received one marked "Urgent".

He opened the message and immediately called Jane Teacher. She was Jessica's daughter and had been running the research lab since Jessica's death fifteen years earlier. He asked Jane to bring Vince with her to his office. When they arrived Jeffery said, "Please sit down. I just received a very disturbing message from Earth. They need our help. Vince, I'm sure you've heard of Yellowstone National Park, correct?"

"Of course. I went there on vacation a few times with my parents. It's a fascinating place."

"Yes, it is, and this fascinating place sits on top of the largest and most active volcanic area on Earth. The message I received said that they are predicting a major volcanic eruption coupled with the largest earthquake ever measured sometime in the next two years. Unless it can be prevented, as many as a billion people will be killed in the event. They want us to help them stop it. The president of the North American Union has sent a scientist here to discuss this with us. He should be here in a few days."

Vince said, "I have no idea how to stop an Earthquake. Do either of you?"

Jane said, "Volcanic eruptions are caused by pressure generated by large quantities magma. If we can find a way to relieve the pressure it might prevent the eruption and the corresponding quake."

136

"Something tells me saying it is a lot easier than doing it. I don't think we could just drill a big hole to take care of the problem," Vince said.

"I'm sure you're correct, drilling a big hole won't help. But I'm confident that between the two of you you'll come up with a solution. This is now your top priority project," Jeffery said.

Jane and Vince left Jeffery's office and walked back to the lab together. Jane was, in Vince's opinion, the most intelligent being in the galaxy. Jane's mother, Jessica, was the most intelligent being when she was alive, and all of Jessica's knowledge passed down to Jane. Jane was reading by the time she was about four months old and continued educating herself by reading every text book she could find. Now, at the age of twenty-one, she was a walking encyclopedia. But she wasn't just knowledgeable, she knew how to apply the knowledge she had to solve the most complex problems. He was sure that if anyone could figure out how to stop a volcano from erupting, it was Jane.

As they walked into the lab Jane said, "Since we can't drill a hole to release the pressure without creating an eruption, maybe we could move the magma to another location?"

"You mean with a transporter? That's only capable of moving something that weighs, at the most, five hundred pounds. Additionally, the range is limited to one hundred units, and that's through space. I have no idea what the range would be through solid material."

"You're right, there are limitations to the current transporters, but that doesn't mean we couldn't improve their capabilities. Anyway, it was just a thought."

"Could we drill sideways into the magma chamber, giving it a different path?"

"That's also a possibility. If I remember correctly, Yellowstone is about a thousand units east of the Pacific Ocean. We could outfit a submarine with a drill of some kind and drill down and east into the chamber to release the magma into the ocean."

"We would have to invent a drill capable of drilling through more than a thousand units of soil and rock, but that might be an easier task then modifying the transporter."

"Let's think about both ideas tonight and we'll discuss it in the morning."

Vince said, "That sounds reasonable." Then he looked at the time display on his communicator and said, "I have a dinner date with Sybil in an hour, so I'm going to go home and get ready. I'll see you in the morning."

"Okay, have a good time."

The next morning Jane and Vince were both in their lab by eight o'clock. They both thought about the suggestions and Jane said, "I think your idea is better. It's easier to implement and would take far less time to build. What do you think?"

"I thought about both proposals. I agree that modifying the transporter is a very complex task and it might take too long to accomplish. If we had ten years instead of two I think it would be a better choice. I can think of a lot of applications for an improved transporter. Other than mining, or road building, I don't think there would be a lot of practical applications for the drill."

"Okay, let's work up a preliminary plan for the drill. I'd like to have something to show the representative from Earth when he gets here."

Jane and Vince spent the entire day discussing different ideas for the drill. The drill had to create a self-sealing shaft to prevent the shaft from collapsing. The only way to do that effectively was to melt the shaft walls. They tested some high-powered lasers to see if they were capable of melting soil and rock into a hard surface, but the lasers were incapable of generating the heat required. Testing indicated that only a fission or fusion reaction would be able to generate the heat required for the task.

They spent the next day thinking about ways to create a controlled nuclear reaction, and by the end of the day they had an idea of how to build their device. The scientist from Earth was due to arrive the following afternoon, so in the morning they created a preliminary design for the device.

Vince and Jane were there to greet Dr. Grant when he arrived. Dr. Grant saw them as soon as he was off the shuttle. He walked over and said, "Good afternoon, I'm Richard Grant. Since you are here to meet me, President Mason must have sent you a message saying I was coming."

Jane said, "It's a pleasure to meet you. I'm Jane Teacher. I manage the research and development area on Procolt 2, and this is my assistant, Vince Kingsley. We did receive a message about your visit. Also, we know the purpose for your visit. Vince and I have been working on possible solutions to the problem. If you would like to accompany us to our lab we can share the progress we have made so far."

"You've actually made some progress! Our people on Earth said it couldn't be done and wouldn't even consider trying. Obviously, I made the right choice when I asked the President about coming here."

"Richard, we don't believe there's any problem that can't be resolved. We came up with two possible solutions, but eliminated one because we were not sure we would be able to finish within the two year time frame. The solution we chose requires no new technology, but using current technology in a different way. Do you want to check in before you come to the lab?"

"No, let's go to the lab. I'm very anxious to see what you have come up with."

Although everyone who comes to Procolt 2 knows about the squirrels, they still find it amazing that a squirrel could hold a meaningful conversation. All the other passengers on the shuttle

139

watched and listened to Jane and Richard's conversation, although they had no idea what they were discussing.

Jane led the way to the lab, and once inside they went to a conference room. At the front of the room was a large video monitor that displayed an image of the west central part of North America. Vince walked to the front of the room by the monitor, Richard sat down on one of the chairs, and Jane climbed up on a chair and stood facing the monitor.

Vince said, "The approach we decided to take to resolve this problem is to dig a tunnel from a point a thousand units west of Yellowstone into the magma pool and allow the magma to flow into the ocean. That would eliminate the pressure building up in the pool."

Richard looked skeptical and asked, "How are you going to make a tunnel a thousand units long?"

"With our fusion drill," Vince responded.

"What is a fusion drill?" Richard asked.

"It's something Vince and I are working on. It's a small fusion reactor mounted on a robotically controlled underwater vehicle. The tip of the drill is four feet in diameter and the reactor heats it to about four thousand degrees. This design will allow the drill to melt the material in front of it and harden the surface of the tunnel so the walls won't collapse. It's still pretty early in the design process, but we think we can drill twenty units per day."

"We don't know the exact location of the magma pool. Won't that have to be located first?" Richard asked.

"Yes, but I'm sure your people are capable of finding it. We'll also need a submarine to act as a base of operations during the drilling process."

"You're right. I'm positive our mining engineers can figure out a way to locate the magma pool. How long do you think it will take you to build the drill?"

Jane answered, "About one hundred twenty days."

"I'll send a message to the president as soon as I get into my room asking him to assign someone to get a team together to locate the magma pool."

Jane asked, "We have a preliminary design for the fusion drill. Would you be interested in looking at it?"

"Yes, I would. I'd like to review it this evening and we can discuss it tomorrow. Is that okay?"

Jane handed him a piece of paper and said, "This is the file name and password for the fusion drill design file. Of course, we can discuss the design tomorrow. Have a good evening Richard. Vince and I are usually in the lab by eight o'clock, but you don't have to be here that early. This is a great place to relax and you should take advantage of it."

Richard said, "It's going to be difficult for me to relax when the lives of a billion people are at risk. I'll be here at eight." Then he left the lab to go check in.

Richard arrived at the lab a few minutes after eight. Jane and Vince were already there. Richard said, "Good morning. Jane, you were right, this is a great place to relax. When all this is over I'm going to come back with my wife and spend a month here. I spent a few hours going over the design and I think it's very clever. I don't see any reason why it won't work. Do you already have the components to build it?"

"I believe we do, but all the components are available to purchase from Coplent. We could have them in six days. I think all three of us should review the design today and I'll check our inventory for parts when we're finished."

Richard said, "Okay, let's get started."

The three of them spent the day going over the design. Richard could not believe how intelligent and knowledgeable Jane was. As they were reviewing the design Jane saw every flaw before Richard or Vince. By the end of the day the design had been

141

modified slightly, but all three of them were convinced it was correct.

Jane cautioned, "I know the design is complete and it looks reasonable, but until we have a working device, we have to assume there will be failures, and we should be prepared for them. If all the parts are in stock we can start building the electronic parts of the device tomorrow. I'll send the drawing over to our metal working group so they can start on the housing for the device. I don't know how long that will take, but probably not more than four or five days. I would hope to have the device built in two weeks. Richard, are you going to stay or are you going back to Earth?"

"If the president will let me, I'll stay here until we know the device works."

"We're going to have to test it on Earth because it will have to be tested under water and controlled from a submarine. We don't have any submarines on Procolt 2."

"I'll arrange everything."

That evening Richard sent a status report to the president and asked if he could stay until the device was finished. After the message was sent he received a message from the University of Montana. It said, "A new analysis of the situation at Yellowstone has just been completed. It was done because we are now experiencing a swarm of quakes and all of them are over 2.5. The analysis indicates that we'll have only twenty months until the super quake occurs."

Richard read the message twice. Then he called Jane and told her about it. She said the shortened time frame means that they will have to increase the power of the device so they can go at least thirty units per day.

They were all in the lab at eight o'clock again the next morning. Jane said, "I spent the night thinking about the design. We were originally going to use one large fusion reactor to heat a

142

four foot diameter area. Now I think we should use four smaller fusion reactors. Each one heating a two foot diameter area, overlapping with the adjacent areas so there is continuous coverage. My calculations indicate that this would allow us to increase the drill speed by fifty percent, allowing us to go thirty units per day. If we only have to go twelve hundred units, and I think that figure is accurate, it would only take forty days to complete the tunnel."

It took the rest of the day to complete the drawings. The next morning Jane sent the new case design over to the metal shop for fabrication and she checked their parts inventory. Everything was in stock except for two small fusion reactors, so she ordered them from her supplier on Coplent.

They started assembling the electronic components immediately. When the finished case arrived four days later, Vince and Jane began mounting the components into the case. The fusion reactors were converted into small rocket engines. The exhaust gases produced by the reactors were very hot, almost four thousand degrees. The reactors were mounted so their exhaust ports were protruding slightly from the front of the device. Each reactor would create a two foot diameter circle of heated plasma fifteen inches from the front of the device.

It took ten days to complete the construction of the fusion drill. The device was about seven feet long. It was basically a three and half foot diameter metal tube that was surrounded by rows of casters that would allow it to travel smoothly through a four foot diameter hole. On the front were the four fusion reactor exhaust ports, and on the back there was a large propeller and a directional control mechanism that would allow the fusion drill to be piloted through water.

Richard sent a message to the president regarding the status of the device and reminding him they needed the use of a submarine for testing. The day after the fusion drill was ready to

143

be tested he received a response that said a submarine had been placed on permanent assignment for Richard's use.

Jeffery and Debbie had been looking for a reason to get away for a while, so they offered to take the team and the fusion drill to Earth on their ship. The following morning the three passengers, the fusion drill, Debbie, and Jeffery were on board the ship and ready to go. There were also several boxes of spare parts and the equipment necessary to diagnose any problems that might arise.

The trip to Earth would take three days. This time they were not stopping at the space station. Instead, Jeffery was going to land at the Treasure Island Naval Station near San Francisco. The submarine they were going to use was based there and would be ready to depart as soon as the fusion drill and the three passengers were on board.

When Jeffery's ship arrived at Treasure Island the base commander was there to greet them. As they got off the ship he said, "Good afternoon. I'm Commander Portman. It's a pleasure to meet all of you. Unfortunately, I have to report some troubling news. While you were in transit from Procolt 2 another swarm of quakes struck the Yellowstone basin. This time several of the quakes were over 4.0 and the president ordered Yellowstone and Grand Teton closed to visitors. Many of the roads through Yellowstone were severely damaged, and two bridges were considered unsafe. The only way to travel to Yellowstone now is by helicopter."

Jeffery said, "I don't believe we're needed, so Debbie and I are going to take a short vacation here before we go back to Procolt 2. Good luck, and if you need anything from us let me know."

Richard was sure their timeframe was reduced again. He did some quick calculations in his head and said, "Jane, based on this information, I think we have less than a year. Perhaps, a lot less."

Jane replied, "I agree. We must begin testing as soon as possible. Have they calculated the best place to start drilling?"

Commander Portman looked at Jane as she spoke. He clearly found her appearance somewhat disconcerting. A few moments later he answered, "Yes, I received those coordinates yesterday. The sub can be there in three days. The starting point is estimated to be seventeen hundred miles from the magma pool. That's about fourteen hundred units."

Richard said, "Then we shouldn't waste time. Let's get going as soon as possible!"

The base commander said, "I agree. Jane, I do want to caution you about something. The men on board have never seen an intelligent squirrel and I don't know how they will react to you. I hope they don't do anything to offend you, but it's possible."

"Commander Portman, I do understand and I won't be offended. Although I have never been to Earth before, I have been to Coplent several times. When I walk with humans there the locals think I'm a pet. If they stare at me I usually say, 'Hi, my name is Jane. Is there something I can help you with?' They are invariably surprised I can speak fluently. Then they get embarrassed and turn away."

"That's a clever way to handle it. I'll have all the material you brought moved to the sub. It should be ready to go in an hour."

As the three of them boarded the sub several of the men on board gawked at Jane, but nobody said anything. The Captain of the sub greeted them as they got on board, "Welcome aboard. I'm Captain Marshall."

He handed each of them a small communicator and said, "These communicators are for you to use while you are on the boat. They have been programmed with your first names. To use them just push the green button and say the name of the person you want to speak to. You can also use a title. For example, if you want to speak to me you can say 'Chuck' or 'Captain'."

Jane took the communicator from the Captain and looked at it. She was somewhat surprised to see her picture on the back. She said, "Thank you Captain, it's a pleasure to be here."

Jane, Vince, and Richard followed the Captain to the officer's area of the sub. Each of them had their own cabin. The cabins were small, but fully equipped. There was a bed, a dresser, a small closet, a desk, and a private bath. When the Captain showed Jane her room he said, "I hope this is okay. The room was obviously designed for humans, but if you need anything to make yourself more comfortable don't hesitate to ask. I suspect you're going to be here for a long time, so if it's necessary I can have my men make any alterations you need."

"Thank you, Captain, but that won't be necessary. I think the only thing I will need will be a waterproof stool that I can stand on in the shower."

"I'll have one brought over. Anything else?"

"Yes, we need a space to set up the control equipment for the fusion drill."

"We've already cleared out a space for you in the officer's mess area. We put some work tables in there and a few chairs. If you have any special power requirements let me know immediately."

"We brought our own power modules, so electrical power won't be a problem. Please ask your men to move all the equipment we brought to that area and we'll set it up and test it shortly."

"Do you need the fusion drill too, or can I place it in the hold until we get onsite?"

"As long as we have access to it, that will be acceptable."

"I'll make sure it's placed so you'll have the access you'll need. We should be ready to leave in an hour."

146

A half hour later all the control equipment was in the officer's mess. Richard and Vince began unpacking everything and putting it on the work table the Captain provided. Jane was too small to lift anything, but she immediately began connecting all the control units together. Two officers were sitting drinking coffee and watching the three of them working. They appeared to be amused as they watched Jane, but they didn't say anything.

Just as the last piece of equipment was placed on the table there was an announcement that said the boat would be departing in five minutes. Captain Marshall walked up to them and asked, "Are any of you interested in watching our departure from the deck?"

Richard responded, "Thank you for the offer Captain, but we have a few more hours of work to get all this stuff wired together. Then we're going to test the controls and make sure the fusion drill propulsion system is working properly. I suspect we'll be working for the next seven or eight hours."

"Okay, by the way, if you want something to eat or drink just ask the chef. He'll get you whatever you want."

"Thank you, Captain. I'm sure we'll all take advantage of that shortly."

Then Captain Marshall asked, "Jane, do you need a special diet?"

"I eat fruits and vegetables. I drink water, coffee, and occasionally soft drinks. I don't need anything special. Thank you for your concern, Captain."

"You're welcome. I just received a message from President Mason that stated this submarine and its crew are available to provide any assistance you may need to complete your task. So, please don't hesitate or think you are bothering us. If you need anything, just ask."

"Okay Captain, we understand. For now, we're fine. We'll probably need some assistance when we start testing the drill's

147

drive mechanism. If we do, I'll contact you immediately," Richard said.

Six hours later they were ready to test the drive mechanism, but took a break for dinner first. After dinner Richard called the Captain and told him they were ready to begin testing and he needed somebody handy with tools. The Captain said he would have someone there in a few minutes.

Five minutes later a man carrying a toolbox walked into the officer's mess. He looked around and saw Vince standing in front of the table with all the control equipment. He walked up to Vince and said, "Hi, I'm Machinist Mate Dennis Crawford. The Captain sent me over to help you."

Vince said, "I need you to take me to the hold where the fusion drill is stored. We will have to uncrate it and open it so I can connect the power module. Can you help me with that?"

"Yes sir."

"Okay Dennis, lead the way."

It took Vince and Dennis an hour to unpack the fusion drill and connect the power module. When it was done Vince called Jane and told her they were ready.

Jane said, "I'll run the standard tests first. Is the prop clear?"

"Yes, you can start whenever you're ready."

The propeller began to rotate and the directional control mechanism began to go through a series of gyrations. The test took two hours. When it was finished Richard and Jane went over the reports. Everything looked good. The following day they were going to test the communication system.

They all met in the officer's mess at eight o'clock the next morning. Captain Marshall saw them as they walked in and asked, "How are things going?"

Jane replied, "The propulsion system tests ran perfectly. Today we're going to check the communication system. We're going to keep reducing the power to the transmitter to simulate long distance communication. This will determine if we'll need repeaters in the tunnel. After we finished last night I was thinking about what happens when we penetrate the wall enclosing the magma pool. The fusion drill is designed to withstand temperatures in excess of three thousand degrees, so it wouldn't be damaged by exposure to the magma alone. However, we have no idea what the pressure is inside the magma pool. If the pressure is very high, the magma may be forced out through the hole at speeds approaching a thousand units per hour. That would probably destroy the control mechanism and the drill would be stuck in the tunnel, effectively trapping the magma."

"Okay, so what do you suggest?"

"I think we need to use an explosive and not the drill to break into the magma pool."

"Can the drill carry it there?"

"With some modifications, yes. I'll get started on that immediately. How big would the explosive device be?"

"We have some small torpedoes. They are four and a half feet long and five inches in diameter, and can be fit with an explosive capable of demolishing a rock wall ten feet thick and four feet in diameter."

"Is the case of the torpedo magnetic?"

"Yes."

"That would be perfect, Captain. Thank you."

Jane climbed up on a chair in front of one the computers and began working on the design changes. Vince and Richard began testing the communications system.

Two hours later Jane had finished the design modifications. There was now a five foot long and six inch wide slit in the wall of drill with a remote controlled removeable cover over the slit. Inside were three powerful electromagnets. The magnets would hold the torpedo firmly in place until it was ready to be dropped.

She printed out the drawing of the modified case and the formula for the metal alloy used to make the case of the fusion drill. Then she called the Captain.

When the Captain answered she said, "Captain, we need to make a new case for the fusion drill. I have the plans ready. However, the case has to be made from a special alloy. I have the formula for that also. We need this done as soon as possible."

"I'll come over and pick up the plans. Then I'll contact the president. I'm positive we'll have someone working on this immediately."

Jane told Vince about changes that were needed. He told her he would have them finished in four hours after the communications tests were completed. The results of the communications tests were inconclusive. The probability they would be able to communicate with the fusion drill through fourteen hundred units of rock was sixty-two percent. They couldn't take the chance. Something would have to place repeaters every two hundred units in the tunnel. Jane would have to discuss that with the Captain. They had all lost track of time. It was almost ten o'clock, and none of them had eaten dinner. So, Jane decided to wait until the morning to discuss the communication problem. Vince had the wiring and circuit changes finished in the timeframe he promised.

The next morning Vince started working on the modifications to the fusion drill's electronics and made the electromagnets from parts he found on the sub. Jane contacted the Captain and asked for a meeting. The Captain told her to come to his cabin.

When she got there the door was open so she walked in. Captain Marshall was seated at a small table and said, "Good morning Jane, would you like something to drink?"

"No, thank you. Since we have been on board things have not gone as smoothly as I had hoped. The results of the communication test indicated that in order to insure the success of this mission we will need to install signal repeaters every two hundred units. That will have to be done by something other than the drill."

"I have several programable submersibles on board. I'm certain they could be programmed to place the repeaters. I'll discuss this with my chief engineer, but I don't think it's a problem. I thought you should know that the new case will be finished sometime today and they will bring it to us at the drill site tomorrow morning by helicopter. We will be at the drill site by eleven o'clock tomorrow morning. How long do you think it will take to move the components into the new case?"

"Probably two days. I know that puts us a day behind schedule, but there was no way I could predict the density of the rock in this area before we got here. I did my calculation based on the soil on Procolt 2, but the soil on Earth has a much higher iron content and is more resistant to radio signals."

I don't think losing a day will make a big difference. There have been no reports of unusual seismic activity in the Yellowstone basin in the last few days. At least we know things have not gotten worse."

"Captain, I believe that our timeline is critical. Richard and I both agree we probably have less than a half year before the eruption occurs. Every day we lose is critical."

"I understand, and I would like this completed as soon as possible too. If any of my men can be of assistance to you, please let me know."

"The only thing I will need is for your men to put the drill into the water as soon as it's mounted in its new case."

"Just contact me whenever you're ready. I'm sure we will have it in the water in a half hour."

The sub arrived at the drill site a half hour earlier than scheduled. At eleven o'clock a helicopter was approaching the sub and landed a few minutes later on the deck. Three crewmen from the sub removed the new drill case from the helicopter and took it to officer's mess. Vince, Richard, and Dennis unpacked the drill case from the crate and Vince immediately began checking it. After a half hour he said the case was made correctly and the process of moving the drill components into the case began.

After two eighteen hour days the redesigned fusion drill was ready for testing. The testing took three hours and was completely successful. Jane called the Captain and told him they were ready to put the drill in the water.

The starting point for the tunnel was at a depth of one hundred ten feet. The sub dove to the correct depth and was positioned fifty feet from the starting point. Three divers took the drill out of the sub and moved it into position.

Jane powered on the propulsion system on the drill and it began to move forward slowly. A problem was detected almost immediately. There was a four knot current over the drill site and the directional control system was unable to compensate for it. Jane called the Captain and explained the problem.

Captain Marshall replied, "The divers are still in the water. Would it be safe for them to hold the drill until the first few feet of the tunnel were drilled?"

"I'm not sure. I don't want to injure anyone. I think it would be safe as long as they were ten feet from the drill."

"I can have the machine shop make some ten foot metal poles. The divers can use them to hold the drill in place while you start the tunneling process."

"That's a good idea Captain. How long will it take to make the poles?"

"Probably less than two hours. I'll contact them now. Do we need to bring the drill back on board?"

"No, I can keep it roughly in the same position until the poles are ready."

"Good, I'll call you as soon as they are ready."

The poles were ready in less than an hour. The divers who came back on board to wait for the poles left the sub again, each of them armed with a ten foot steel pole. The end of each pole was fitted with a small hook that could be hooked around the casters that surrounded the drill case.

Jane moved the drill close to the rock wall and the divers moved it into position so that the front of the drill was touching the wall. Jane powered on the fusion reactors up to fifty percent power. Instantly the rock wall in front of the drill began to disintegrate. The divers kept the drill steady as it slowly penetrated the rock. A few minutes later the tunnel was five feet deep. Jane turned off the drill. The divers unhooked the poles and returned to the sub.

Jane restarted the drill and this time brought the power level in the reactors up to seventy-five percent. The drill began to move forward. The drill's path was already programmed into the control unit and after fifteen minutes the tunnel was two thousand feet long. The drill was working perfectly. Jane notified Captain Marshall, and Richard sent a message to President Mason.

The drill was now beginning to move slightly downward and would continue on the same path until it was at a depth of twenty-seven units. Then it would go east, directly toward the magma pool.

Jane, Vince, and Richard were all taking eight hour shifts monitoring the drills progress, but there wasn't really much to do. The drill was doing the job, they just had to keep watch in case something went wrong.

After forty-eight hours the tunnel was sixty units long. Jane called the Captain. When he answered she said, "Captain Marshall, the drill is still functioning as expected. The tunnel is now sixty units long. I think it's time to prepare the first submersible. I'm sure it's significantly faster than the drill, but I would like to have the repeater in place shortly after the drill passes the two hundred unit point."

"The submersible travels at about fifty miles per hour, so it can go two hundred units in about five hours. Tomorrow we'll prepare it for launch and launch it the next day. The submersible can hold ten repeaters, a few more than we need. We'll drop one on the bottom of the tunnel every two hundred units."

The submersible was launched on schedule and dropped its first repeater just over two hundred units into the tunnel. Things were going very smoothly until thirty-two days after the launch. Vince was watching the images coming from the drill when the image began jumping. Something was shaking the drill violently. Vince turned off the fusion generators and backed up the drill so he could have a better view of the end of the tunnel. The rock at the end of the tunnel appeared to be moving. It had to be an Earthquake. If the tunnel collapsed behind the drill the project would fail. The shaking stopped about twenty seconds after it started. Vince switched the view to the rear camera and the tunnel appeared to be intact, but it only showed the area twenty feet behind the drill.

Vince picked up his communicator and called Jane. When she answered he said, "We just had another quake. The drill started shaking. The area in front of the drill looks okay. I looked behind the drill and the area right behind it looks normal, but I have no way of knowing if the tunnel behind the drill is still open. The quake lasted about twenty seconds."

"The tunnel is only about four hundred units from the magma pool and I'm sure that's close enough to be affected by a quake in the Yellowstone Basin. I'll call Richard and let him know. I think you should turn the drill back on and continue drilling."

"I was going to do that, but I want to make you aware of the situation first."

It was in the middle of the night but Jane called Richard anyway. He answered the phone by asking, "What?"

"I'm sorry to wake you, but I believe there has been another quake. Vince said the drill started shaking. He's worried that the tunnel may have collapsed behind the drill. Anyway, we have to find out more about that quake."

"I'll make some calls immediately."

Twenty minutes later Richard called Jane and said, "We're in trouble. It was indeed a quake that Vince experienced. It was centered in the Yellowstone Basin and preliminary information is that the quake registered 5.9. They are going to analyze the situation and call me as soon as the analysis is complete, but the guy I talked to said we may have less than fifteen days before the big one."

"You have to inform the president. "We have to drill for another twelve days to reach the magma pool. Then we have to drop the torpedo and back the drill out of the tunnel. It will go much faster, but it will still take ten days to back out."

"Were still running the drill at seventy-five percent power. If we increase the power we may be able to cut two or three days off the drilling time."

"Yes, but that also increases the risk of some kind of failure. I don't want to do that unless we have no choice. Call me as soon as you get the report."

It was only five o'clock in the morning when Richard called President Mason. Richard identified himself to the man who answered the phone and said he had to speak the president immediately. A minute later the president was on the phone. He said, "I assume this is very important Richard, otherwise you're fired."

"I'll let you make the decision. There was another quake in the Yellowstone Basin about an hour ago. It was the strongest one yet, and preliminary estimates show the quake was 5.9 on the

155

Richter scale. Vince was watching the drill when it started shaking violently, so our operation was affected. The guy I spoke to at the university said he thought the big one might occur in less than fifteen days. We need twelve days to finish drilling and ten days to back the drill out of the tunnel."

"Okay, you're not fired. Is there anything you can do to speed up the process?"

"We are only running the drill at seventy-five percent power. We could increase it to full power and that would probably shave two or three days off the drilling time, but Jane is concerned that it would also increase the possibility of a failure. The drill is a very complex device, and if it fails there is no way to finish the task in time."

"Wow! It sounds like we're screwed. Are they certain about the reduced timeframe?"

"No, they're analyzing the data now. They will call me as soon as it's complete."

"And you will call me the moment you hear anything."

"Yes sir, I'll do that."

Two hours later Richard received a call from the university. The man who called said, "Richard, the quake was more powerful than we originally thought. We now think it was a 6.1. More worrisome is that the system predicted there is a seventy-one percent probability that in eighteen days Yellowstone will explode for the first time in more than six hundred thousand years. The quake six hundred thousand years ago was probably the most powerful one that ever occurred on Earth. This next one may be hundreds of times more powerful."

Richard was unable to speak for several seconds. The situation was far worse than he ever expected. He finally said, "I wish the news was better, but thank you for the information. I have some calls to make," and he ended the call.

Richard called Jane and gave her the bad news. She thought for a moment and said, "Let's increase the drill to ninety-five percent. I also had an idea. I think I may be able to cause the fusion reactors to explode and destroy the drill. That way it wouldn't block the magma flow."

"Yes, but an explosion twenty-seven units underground could create an Earthquake."

"I realize that's a possibility, but it would be far smaller than the one predicted for Yellowstone."

"We really don't have a choice."

Jane called Vince and said, "I just got word on the quake you noticed. It was a 6.1 quake in the Yellowstone Basin. The computer models indicate the big quake will occur in eighteen days. At the speed the drill is currently going, it will take us twelve days to reach the magma pool. We have to cut that time by as much as possible. Increase the power to the reactors to ninety-five percent and push the drill as fast as you can."

"If we only have eighteen days and we use ten of them to get to the magma pool, that only leaves us eight days to back the drill out of the tunnel. There's no way we can do it that fast."

"I know, I'm working on that now."

Vince increased the power to the reactors as Jane requested. After two hours the tunnel length was increased by almost two units, a twenty-five percent increase in forward speed. Richard took over for Vince a few minutes later. Vince told him about the increase in speed. They both said they hoped it would be enough.

Before Jane took over she completed the programming necessary to cause the fusion reactors in the drill to explode and loaded the program into the control computer. Once the program was executed, the drill would explode in less than two minutes.

Nine days later the drill's job was completed. They were close enough to the magma pool that the surface temperature on the rock in front of the drill was three hundred forty-one degrees. They dropped the torpedo in the tunnel and began backing the drill out.

Jane notified the Captain and told him he should be prepared to fire the torpedo at a moment's notice. He said he would keep the launch control switch with him at all times.

The actual length of the tunnel was thirteen hundred eighty-seven units. The drill was traveling backwards through the tunnel at sixteen units per hour. At that rate, it would take eighty-seven hours to back the drill completely out of the tunnel. If the prediction for the quake was correct, the drill would be out of the tunnel a few days before the quake.

Twenty-eight hours later the drill was just past the position it was in when the last quake occurred. Just as Vince had feared, the tunnel was partially collapsed. The camera showed a layer of loose rock a foot high blocking the tunnel. There was no way for the drill to get past that point. It was designed to travel on smooth surfaces.

Jane called Captain Marshall and asked him to come to the drill control area. When he arrived she said, "We have a problem," and she showed him the tunnel.

While the Captain was looking at the monitor Jane said, "The pile of rocks appears to be about a foot high and several feet deep. The drill will not be able to move through that, so it's basically stuck at its current position."

"Which is where?" the Captain asked.

"It's four hundred fifty units west of the magma pool, under the Columbia Plateau in eastern Oregon."

"Are there any populated areas there?"

"The closest city is Burns, and that's about fifty units west and twenty units south of the drill's position."

"Is the area geologically stable? If we blow up the drill, will it cause a quake?"

"Probably, but I think it would be a small one, less than 5.0. But, that's a guess. There's no way to accurately predict what will happen. It's also possible that there is sufficient area in front of the drill to relieve the pressure in the magma pool."

"I'm not prepared to make this decision," Captain Marshall said. Then he turned toward Richard and said, "Richard, you have to contact President Mason. This has got to be his decision."

Richard went to the phone and placed a call to the president. They had a brief conversation. Richard came back and said, "The president wants to discuss this with some of his advisors before he makes his decision. He said he would call me back in a few hours.

However, the next call Richard received was not from the president. It was from the Lab at the University of Montana. The man, petrified with fear, told Richard that a new swarm of more powerful quakes had just started. He said the big quake would occur within minutes.

Richard hung up the phone and yelled, "Captain, set off the torpedo now!"

The Captain took the torpedo fire control switch out of his pocket and activated the torpedo. Then the Captain looked at Jane and said, "There's no time to wait for the president to make a decision. Blow the drill."

Jane typed in a command and said, "In two minutes the drill will explode."

Then the Captain asked, "Won't the explosion collapse the tunnel?"

"Yes, but it will also create a huge pocket where the drill is currently located. I believe that the pocket will have sufficient area to hold the magma that comes through the tunnel. Richard, I think you should call the university and find out what's happening."

Before Richard could get to the phone it rang. Richard answered it. It was the same man who had called a few minutes

159

earlier. This time he said, "The swarm of quakes stopped. Did you do something?"

"Yeah, we opened the tunnel to the magma pool. The magma should be flowing out of the chamber and through the tunnel."

"But you didn't have time to get the drill out of the tunnel. What did you do?"

"We blew it up."

"Was the drill under eastern Oregon?"

"Yes."

"That explains the quake that just occurred there."

"How strong was the quake?"

"The preliminary estimate is 4.8."

"Is that strong enough to cause any damage on the surface?"

"Yeah, but in that area there is nothing to damage."

"Good, please keep me posted on this."

"Sure, I'll call you back in fifteen minutes."

Richard walked back to the group, and with a big smile on his face, said, "It appears that our mission was a complete success!"

Captain Marshall looked at Richard, Vince, and Jane and said, "You have just saved the lives of millions of people. I don't know how we can ever thank you."

Jane said, "We were just doing our jobs. No thanks are necessary."

The Captain said, "I'm sure President Mason won't feel that way."

That evening, on a worldwide broadcast, President Mason told the world about the problem, and that due to the efforts of two scientists from Procolt 2 and one of his science advisors, the lives of perhaps a billion people were saved.

160

Two days later, at a formal dinner at President Mason's residence, the president personally thanked them for their efforts and gave each of them a medal. It was the first time a squirrel had ever been so honored.

Procolt 2

When Jane and Vince returned to Procolt 2 they went to see Jeffery. He already knew the mission was a complete success, but they wanted to talk to him about the fusion drill. They found him in the restaurant, at his favorite table in the back, drinking a cup of coffee.

Jeffery saw them coming, and when they were by the table he said, "Congratulations, you both did an excellent job."

Jane said, "Thank you, but I think there was some luck involved too. Anyway, we wanted to talk to you about the fusion drill."

"I've been thinking about it too. I think it would be a very useful product to build. I'm positive every member of the trade group would buy them to build roads and use for mining operations. We could probably sell thousands of them every year."

Jane said, "That is exactly what we were discussing on the way back from Earth. There's an empty building in New Paris that would be a perfect place to manufacture them."

"Yes, I'm aware of that. Why the sudden interest in manufacturing? I thought you were more concerned with the technical aspects of the things we do here."

"I'll admit I have an ulterior motive. I want money to build a small city for the squirrels. There are now almost ten thousand of us, and we are spread out in small groups all over. I would like to build one location for all of us to live."

"You should know me well enough by now to realize that all you had to do was ask and I would have given you anything you wanted."

"I know, but I didn't want charity. I wanted to earn the money, and I think this will do it."

"I'm sure you're correct. Where do you want to build this city?"

"Not far away. Most of us work here and I want the commute times to be reasonable."

"Do you want me to hire an architect to work with you or do you want to design it yourself?"

"Actually, I've already spoken to Justin Younger about it. He should have the plans completed by now."

"Why don't you and Justin find a location and then set up a meeting with me? I'd like to see what you want to build. As far as manufacturing the fusion drills is concerned, I think you should finish the designs and then, if the building is still available in New Paris, we'll turn it into a manufacturing facility. If it has been spoken for, we can always build a new building."

Vince, who had been quiet up till now said, "I think we need three different size devices, based on the diameter of the tunnel. I would suggest we build ten foot, thirty foot, and fifty foot models."

"That seems reasonable. Remember, they have to be able to fit in the hold of a ship, unless you want to assemble them on site."

Vince responded, "Since the designs aren't even started we don't know how big the finished product will be, but we'll make certain not to create a shipping problem."

Jane said, "It will take thirty days or more to finish the designs. I'll let you know when they are ready. Also, I'll contact Justin and find out if the habitat plans are completed. I'll meet with him and make sure I'm happy with them before we set up a meeting."

"Perfect," Jeffery replied.

Ten days later Jeffery received a call from Jane telling him the plans for the new squirrel habitat were finished and she was very happy with the results. A meeting was set up for the following afternoon.

163

In addition to Jeffery, Debbie, Jane, and Justin, the supervisor of Jeffery's construction crew, Derick Tremble, was also invited to the meeting. Justin presented the plans and everyone in the room was very impressed. The habitat was more like a city. There were places that dispensed food, medicine, and clothing. The squirrels did not usually wear clothes, but many of them liked to wear shoes, hats, and gloves. Also, some of the jobs they worked in required them to wear protective clothing.

There were three thousand apartments, each capable of housing a family of up to six. There were moving sidewalks everywhere, so the squirrels could get where they needed to go quickly. There was also an automated tram system that would take them to Procolt Paradise.

When the presentation of the plans was finished, Justin showed an aerial view of the construction area. It was located twenty units northeast of Procolt Paradise. The area was currently a large flat meadow, dotted with trees, and there were three small rivers flowing through the intended construction area.

Jeffery asked, "Derick, what do you think about the design?"

"I like it, and I think it will be easy to build. However, it will probably still take a year to finish. After I have a chance to review the plans more thoroughly I will be able to give you an accurate estimate of time and construction costs."

"Have you picked a name for the place?" Jeffery asked.

Justin responded, "Yes, we naming it after Jane's mother, Jessica. It's going to be called Jessica's Meadow."

Jeffery nodded and said, "That's a wonderful idea. I really like it."

Jane said, "There is something else I wanted to discuss with you. It appears the designs for the fusion drills will take longer than I anticipated. Apparently, the empty factory in New Paris is now spoken for. Procolt Engineering just received a contract to build

164

the control electronics for the ships NASA is building and refurbishing here, and they signed a twenty year lease for the factory. I would like to build a new factory near Jessica's Meadow, and I want the factory to use squirrels as employees."

"Give me a couple of days to think about that."

"Jeffery, the unemployment rate among the humanoid population of Procolt 2 is about one percent. Among squirrels, it's thirteen percent. They need to feel useful. They don't like sitting around doing nothing, and this would give them something to do."

"How many squirrels would you expect to be employed there?"

"It depends on sales, but I would guess about seven hundred fifty."

"That would take care of the unemployment problem."

"Yes, it would."

"Okay, you make a good point. But I still want a day or two to think about it."

"I'm sure you'll come to the correct conclusion. You always do."

Jeffery said, "Derrick please get whatever you need from Justin and report back to me in ten days."

"Okay, that's fine. Tomorrow I'll go out to the proposed site and make sure there aren't any problems."

Jeffery ended the meeting. After everyone was gone Debbie said, "Jeffery, I want this to be your last major project. I think we're both getting too old to do this kind of stuff."

"I'm sorry, but I don't agree. I know we're both over a hundred, but I don't feel any older than I did when we first got here. If you're feeling old it's probably physiological, not physical. Besides, I want to keep active. I don't want to sit around and watch the world go by. However, I won't go looking for new projects, but if one comes along I can't promise you I won't get involved."

Debbie sighed and said, "I suppose that's the best I can hope for."

Ten days later everybody was together again. Derrick opened the meeting by handing out copies of his report and saying, "I've gone over Justin's designs and examined the proposed construction site and I'm very pleased to say everything looks good. As you can see, the cost will be approximately one hundred thousand hirodim. There is something about this project that I'm sure you're not aware of. This will be the first major construction project on Procolt 2 that will not require us to import any materials from another planet. We now manufacture everything that will be needed. That means that the entire cost for the project will go back into the economy of Procolt 2."

Jeffery smiled and said, "That's good news Derrick. I've always wanted Procolt to be as self-sufficient as possible and it's obvious we are moving in that direction."

Derrick continued, "I believe the first phase of the project should be the construction of the tram that runs between Procolt Paradise and the construction site. That will enable the construction workers to get to the site easily. It will also help with getting supplies to the site. I can begin construction of the tram in five days, and it will be completed thirty days later. While the tram is being built, I'll get the equipment and materials needed for the first five buildings brought to the site. I don't have enough people on my staff for this project, so we will need to hire at least two hundred additional people."

Jane asked, "Can any of those positions be filled by squirrels?"

"I hadn't thought about that, but I would guess half of the jobs could be done by squirrels. I'm sure they could handle any task that doesn't require a lot of physical strength."

"I can have a hundred squirrels for you whenever you need them."

"I'll let you know ten days before they'll be needed."

Jeffery said, "I need to discuss this with Debbie before we get started. I want to study Derrick's report. Debbie and I will discuss this tonight and I'll give you my answer tomorrow morning. Thank you all for coming."

Derrick said, "If you have any questions regarding the report please contact me immediately."

"I'll do that. Thank you, Derrick."

After the others left Debbie said, "A hundred thousand hirodim is a lot of money. I know we can afford it, but I thought this project was going to be paid for by sales of the fusion drills."

"I'm sure it will be, but we'll have to put up the money first. Is that your only concern?"

"Probably, but let's talk about it at dinner. I'm hungry."

"Okay."

Jeffery and Debbie both decided to go ahead with the Jessica's Meadow project and the following morning Jeffery contacted Derrick, Justin, and Jane to tell them the project was approved.

Construction of the tram was started five days later. The plan was to build a road from Jessica's Meadow to Procolt Paradise. In the center of the road was an area wide enough for two trams to travel. The trams were basically driverless buses that would travel at fifty units per hour, so the trip would take less than a half hour. The trams would run in a circle continuously and would be spaced one tenth of an hour apart. The road took twenty-five days to build. While the road was being built, a company in Procolt City began building the trams and Derrick's people began constructing the tram stations in Procolt Paradise and Jessica's Meadow.

Six days after the road was completed the first tram began its test run. Jeffery, Debbie, Jane, Derrick, and Justin were all on board the tram for its maiden journey. The trip was quick,

167

comfortable, and without problems. The other trams would be put into service as soon as they were completed.

The designs for the fusion drills took longer than Jane and Vince thought. Jane's original estimate of thirty days was off by more than ninety days. The smallest one would be externally controlled, but the two larger ones were designed to be manually operated. Jane insisted they had to be designed so the size of the person operating the unit was irrelevant. This significantly increased the design time and the manufacturing costs.

At first Jeffery thought the requirement to accommodate any size operator was a waste of time and money. Jeffery had assumed Jane insisted on this so the drills could be operated by a squirrel, but he was wrong.

Jeffery had begun taking orders for the drills before the designs were complete and an order for four units was placed, including two fifty foot models, by the government of Fardrin. Jeffery had never met anyone from Fardrin, but he soon discovered they were humanoids, but the tallest of them was less than four feet.

It took a year to finish Jessica's Meadow, but the first buildings were ready to be occupied sixty days after construction started, and squirrels by the hundreds moved in.
The fusion drill factory was finished forty days after Jessica's Meadow.

When the factory began building fusion drills they started with the fifty foot models, because they represented a majority of the orders. When the first drill was finished it was tested in the factory, and it passed all the tests. Jane wanted a real test so she had the first drill moved to a valley fifty units east of Jessica's Meadow.

The fifty foot model would create a tunnel that was a semicircle, with a fifty foot wide flat base. The drill was an engineering masterpiece. It was forty-eight feet wide and thirty-

168

five feet long. Since this device moved through air, not water, the propulsion system was completely different. It moved on six metal alloy wheels, each wheel powered by its own large electric motor. The movement of each wheel was controlled by a computer that was attached to a joy stick on the operator console. The front of the drill was adorned with twenty-four fusion reactors. Since there was no water to carry away the heat on the sides of the tunnel, the drill drew in large amounts of cooler air from behind it and blew it at the walls of the tunnel to solidify them.

The drill was transported to the test site by a large shuttle. Jane drove it off the shuttle and stopped twenty feet from the mountain. Jeffery, Debbie, Vince, and Derrick were there to watch the test. The observers could hear Jane speak through their com units.

Jane powered up the fusion reactors and said, "Reactors at fifty percent. Moving forward now."

They watched as the drill moved forward and when it just a few inches from the side of the mountain the rock began to glow and melt. Jane said, "Setting forward speed to one half unit per hour."

Slowly the drill moved into the mountain, creating a perfect semicircle. They watched as the mountain engulfed the drill. It seemed to be working perfectly. A quarter of an hour later the drill was a few hundred feet into the mountain. Suddenly there was a loud cracking sound coming from the tunnel. It grew in intensity until it was almost painful. Jeffery screamed into his com unit for Jane to back out of the tunnel, but it too late. It sounded like an explosion when the tunnel collapsed, burying Jane and the drill inside the mountain. There was no way to rescue her; she was gone.

No one said anything, they all just stared at the mountainside where the tunnel had been only a few moments earlier. Finally, Jeffery broke the silence and said, "Vince, you're

169

in charge now. All production stops until we figure out what went wrong. Do you think there is any way to rescue her?"

Vince looked at a monitor and said, "The telemetry indicates she is three hundred fourteen feet inside the mountain. It would take at least ten days to reach her. There is no way she could survive that long."

Then Jeffery began to cry, and said softly, "I'm going to miss her."

Debbie said tearfully, "We all will."

Then Jeffery said, "When we are able to recover her body I want you to give her a proper burial."

Vince said, "Jeffery, I promise you I will do everything I can to recover her body."

Jane never had children, so her knowledge, and Jessica's, was lost forever. Jeffery and Debbie took on the task of finding the most intelligent squirrel on Procolt 2.

After more than thirty days they selected a male named Elliott. He was teaching computer engineering at the school, and seemed to have extensive knowledge about almost everything.

Jeffery met with Elliott to tell him that he had been selected to take over Jane's position and Elliott said he would be proud to follow in her footsteps. Jeffery said his first task was to figure out why the tunnel Jane was drilling collapsed, and what needs to be done to prevent it from happening again.

Elliott nodded and said, "Thank you, sir. I'll get started immediately."

Six days later Jeffery received a call from Elliott. He said, "Sir, I believe that I figured out what happened with the fusion drill. I examined the rock near the cave entrance and found there were large amounts of soft soil mixed in with the rock. I'm certain there is a layer of soft soil under the rock and that soil would not provide adequate support for the rock above. That resulted in the collapse of the tunnel. You should know that there was no way

170

Jane could have known that. Soft soil is very unusual in any mountain on Procolt 2."

"That sounds logical. How do we prevent that from happening again?"

"I think we need to make a small drill that can be used to bore into the rock first and analyze the material we will be drilling through. If we find soft soil we have to change the drilling location or drill until we reach the pocket of soft soil and remove it by using conventional methods. Then as the soft soil is removed we will have to build perimeter supports to prevent the tunnel from collapsing. It may also be possible to make modifications to the drill to handle soft soil if it is detected."

"How long will it take to build the small drill?"

"About thirty days."

"Please start on it immediately. I have orders for more than a hundred drills and although I explained to them the drills will not be delivered for a year, I know they will start getting impatient soon."

"Yes, sir. I understand."

"Elliott, I know this is a personal question but I'm concerned about our research and development lab. When Jane died we lost the knowledge of both Jane and Jessica. I don't want that to happen again. Therefore, I need to ask you something. Have you selected a female partner yet?"

"Yes, I have. We are living together in an apartment in Jessica's Meadow. I believe you interviewed her for the position I was given. Her name is Melody, and she teaches advanced mathematics at the school. I'm not offended by your question. I think it was both reasonable and logical. Also, she told me just a few days ago she is pregnant."

"That's wonderful! Congratulations Elliott!"

"Thank you, sir. Melody is far more knowledgeable in mathematics than I am, so our child will be perfectly suited to manage the lab when the time comes."

"Thank you for that information. Please keep me informed on the status of the small drill."

"Of course. One more thing I thought you should know. The construction on the park and recreation area in Jessica's Meadow is almost finished. At a meeting yesterday we decided to name it Jane Teacher Park. Inside the park we're going to build a memorial for her, and I want you and the other squirrels to design it."

"I think that is a very nice gesture. She was the driving force behind Jessica's Meadow, so I'm glad she'll be remembered. I will discuss the memorial with the other squirrels at our meeting next week."

"Good, and don't concern yourself with the cost. I will take care of it."

"Thank you."

The small fusion drill was ready for testing thirty days later, as Elliott predicted. They took it to the same place where Jane was killed. The drill worked perfectly and confirmed Elliott's thought about soft soil. There was still a problem. Elliott decided that manually drilling in soft soil was still dangerous, so he made the decision to modify the drills to work in a soft soil environment.

It took Elliott and his team another thirty-five days to find a solution to the problem. They developed a plastic resin that could be sprayed onto the cave walls if soft soil was detected. The resin hardened in a few seconds into a smooth surface as strong as a one inch thick steel plate.

They tested the modified drill on the same mountain. This time the drill was controlled remotely. The drill had been fitted with sensors to detect soft soil, and when it was detected the forward speed of the drill was slowed to one quarter unit per hour and the power to the fusion reactors was reduced to twenty-five percent. The resin was sprayed onto the walls a few seconds after the tunnel was formed. This time the test was a complete success.

Jeffery did not want to take any chances, so he told Elliott to run more tests on other mountains over the next twenty days. If all the tests were successful they would begin shipping the drills to customers.

At the end of twenty days only a few minor problems were found, and they were quickly resolved. Shipments of the drills began ten days later.

Elliott and Vince decided that it was now safe to locate and remove Jane's remains so they started on that project immediately. Three days later they reached the fusion drill Jane was driving. It was a tricky maneuver but they managed to clear the debris around the control cabin of the drill and that allowed them access to her body. The drill sustained very little damage, so after Jane's body was removed they managed to free up the drill and back it out of the mountain.

Two days after Jane's body was recovered they held a memorial service for her at Jane Teacher Park. There were more than a thousand squirrels and an equal number of humans at the service.

Jeffery began the memorial service. He said, "It is a sad event that brings us all together here. Today we're going to talk about some of Jane's accomplishments, and there were many. But I think she will be most remembered for the task she and Vince performed on Earth that saved a billion lives. When I communicated with President Mason he was deeply sadden by the news of her passing. Two days ago I received a message from him that said the congress of the North American Union voted unanimously to rename Yellowstone National Park. It is now Jane Teacher National Park."

Jeffery paused because of the loud applause caused by his statement. When the applause died down he continued, "We don't have any national parks on Procolt 2, but we will soon start construction on a memorial for Jane, and it will allow future generations to get to know her. Now I'm going to turn the microphone over to Elliott Teacher, who is following in her footsteps, and that is a very difficult task."

For the next hour, a secession of squirrels and humanoids took turns recounting their experiences with Jane. It was very moving.

The day after the memorial for Jane the squirrels held a meeting to elect a new Leader and Elliott was elected unanimously.

Sixty days after Jane's memorial service, when the Jane Teacher Memorial Pavilion was opened, there was a second memorial service for Jane. The crowd was even bigger than it was for her first one. In addition to the residents of Procolt 2, this one was also attended by all the members of Earth's World Council. President Mason spoke at the service and said the Earth owed a debt to Jane that could never be repaid.

After the drills began to ship, Jeffery and Debbie decided it was time to retire. The management of the lab was turned over to Elliott, and Mystic was in charge of Procolt Paradise.

Vandor

Ten years had passed since the completion of Jessica's meadow, and the squirrel population living there exceeded ten thousand. The humanoid population on Procolt 2 was almost two billion, and the planet now had more than fifteen major cities.

Jeffery and Debbie both retired. Their only task was to greet the new visitors as they arrived. It was Jeffery's turn. He watched as the shuttle from the space station landed.

One of the passengers stepped off the shuttle, looked around, saw Jeffery, and walked over to him. He said, "Hello Jeffery. My name is Vandor. It's very important that you and I have a conversation."

"Okay, Mr. Vandor. What would you like to talk about?"

"First, I'm not Mr. Vandor. Vandor is my entire name, although occasionally I used the name Luther Vandor. What I would like to discuss with you is the past history of this galaxy and your part in its future."

"You look human, but something tells me you're not. Would you like to explain?"

"I look human because I am human. However, I was not born on Earth. I'm from the planet Zandrax. I've been living on Earth for most of the last seventy thousand years."

"Is this a joke? I've never heard of Zandrax."

Vandor put his hand on Jeffery's shoulder. Everything around him seemed to evaporate. All he could see was unending white. A few seconds later Jeffery found himself on a large grassy field. There were tall snowcapped mountains in the distance. At the base of the mountains was a large blue lake. It was beautiful, but the vision he was seeing was not on Procolt. It took him a few seconds to realize where he was. He had been there before, many years earlier. He was in northwestern Wyoming inside Grand Teton National Park. Vandor took his hand off of Jeffery's

175

shoulder. Then he smiled at Jeffery and said, "I believe you now realize this isn't a joke."

"Yes, that was very convincing. Are we really on Earth or is this just an image you're projecting into my mind?"

"We're on Earth. I'm sure you recognize this place."

"I do. I was here a long time ago on a vacation with my parents. Do you have the ability to transport yourself to any location in the galaxy?"

"Only if I have been there before. But the ability it not limited by distance. Zandrax is about four thousand light years from here. I can go there too. That's why I came to Procolt 2 on one of your ships. Now that I've been there it won't be necessary to travel by spaceship."

"You said you've been on Earth for most of the last seventy thousand years. Are you immortal?"

"No, but we don't age at the same rate you do. During our first twenty years or so we age like you, but then the aging process slows down. A few years after that we reach a point where we age at about one day for every ten years. I am the equivalent of somebody who is in his early forties from Earth, although I'm more than seventy-five thousand years old."

"I have a lot of questions I would like to ask you about Earth's history."

"I'm sure you do, and I will be happy to answer them if I can. But we must discuss something else first."

Vandor put his hand on Jeffery's shoulder again. When Jeffery's vision cleared they were back on Procolt 2, near the shuttle landing area. "Why don't we go to the restaurant and talk there?"

Jeffery said, "That would be okay."

They walked to the restaurant and Jeffery went to a booth in the back that was devoid of other people. A few moments after they sat down a waitress walked over to the table and said, "Hello sir, is there something I can get for you?"

"Just coffee for me. Vandor, would you like something?"

"Coffee would be fine."

A minute later the waitress brought two cups and a carafe filled with coffee. Then she said, "Please let me know if you want anything else."

Jeffery said, "Thank you," then turned towards Vandor. He said, "So, what do you want to talk about?"

"First, I think you need some background information. The civilization on Zandrax is, as far as we know, the oldest in this part of the universe. Humans have existed there for more than two billion years. It was decided we would take it upon ourselves to plant the seeds of civilization on any planet we believed would be capable of supporting human life. In our quest to do that we discovered Earth about three hundred fifty million years ago. At that time dinosaurs were the dominate species. There were only a few small mammals. We introduced a few larger mammals similar to the cats and dogs that currently live on Earth. We wanted to see if they could survive. They did more than survive, they flourished. We studied Earth regularly for a while, coming back every few thousand years to see how things were going. It became obvious the climate was cooling and the dinosaurs would probably not be able to adapt to the changing conditions. We decided to let things on Earth happen without our interference. We left and didn't return for about ten million years. By that time the dinosaurs were gone and the climate was beginning to stabilize. We were sure we could bring primates to Earth and they would be able to survive, which is what we did. About a million years ago we began flooding the surface of the Earth with radiation similar to the radiation that is currently on Procolt 2. That radiation caused mutations in the primates, and within a hundred thousand years the first humanoids were born. It took another three hundred thousand years until your

177

ancestors were born. We removed the radiation sources and left Earth on its own. We returned only sporadically for the next few thousand years. When I first came to Earth men were just beginning to live in groups, and they discovered how to use simple tools. They made spears for hunting, and with a little help, discovered how useful fire can be."

"Are you saying you were the one who taught early man how to use fire?"

"Yes, I'm sure they would have figured it out on their own, but it might have taken another thousand years. I watched as civilizations developed and died. It became obvious the humans on Earth had one fatal flaw. That flaw was greed. It didn't matter if it was land, water, gold, or anything else. The people in a position of power always wanted more, and they were willing to kill to get it."

Jeffery thought about what Vandor told him for a few seconds and then said, "I don't think that changed until about one hundred fifty years ago. The invention of the power module seemed to have precipitated a change in the attitude of people all over Earth. Once energy became abundant and cheap we began to focus more on science and medicine and became more satisfied with our lives."

"That was our plan. I made sure Albert Simson discovered the right formula for the silver alloy rod that was the primary component in the power module. I don't know if you realize how many times he said during his interviews with the press how lucky he was to have stumbled across the exact formula for the silver bar."

"I never met him, but his grandson, Brandon, spends about half of his time here and the other half on Earth, but I suppose you already know that.

"There is something else about the people from Zandrax you should know. We've developed the ability to predict major events in the future based on current or recently passed events. We

178

can't predict the actions of a single person, or even a group of people, but we can predict, with about ninety percent accuracy, the actions of an entire planet's population. For example, we knew Crosus would not tolerate the loss of their position in the trade group, but because our ability to predict future events is only about ninety percent correct, we didn't know Crosus would attack the mining operation on Procolt 4, or later attack Earth. We also knew they were going to build some kind of super weapon, but we didn't know what it would be. On the plus side, we were almost positive somebody from Earth would build the resort here with the help of people from Coplent, but we did a little covert manipulation to make sure it happened."

"Why did you want us to build a resort here?"

"It's very simple. We want the people from Earth to continue to slowly mutate until you are our equals. The radiation here on Procolt 2 is similar to the radiation on Zandrax. It may take a thousand generations, but eventually it will happen."

"So, the radiation here is not natural?"

"No, it's not. We put sources of radiation all over the planet about four hundred years ago. Then we made an earlier attempt to populate the planet. We arranged for a ship from Metoba to capture some people from Earth and bring them here about three hundred years ago. They were unable to cope with the changes in their environment. As a result, they all died."

"We know about them. The first day we were here we found the remains of a soldier from Earth in a cave. Later we also found a diary that gave us some information about their ordeal."

"Why did you bring primates to Earth and wait for them to mutate? Why didn't you just populate Earth with people from Zandrax?"

"Because we aren't perfect. We have very strong emotions, and that causes problems. Shortly before I came to Earth there was a war on Zandrax that killed thousands of people. The two sides were fighting over a piece of virtually worthless land. For some unknown reason, we often find ourselves being ruled by our emotions instead of logic. Jeffery, we have a lot more to talk about, but for now, I would like to take advantage of some of the things you offer here. Can we continue this tomorrow afternoon? You can use that time to decide what questions you would like to ask me."

"Of course, would you like to meet here tomorrow afternoon at two?"

"Yes, that will be fine."

Vandor got up and walked over to the check-in area. Jeffery called Debbie and asked her to come down to the main restaurant as soon as possible.

Ten minutes later Debbie walked into the restaurant, saw Jeffery, and walked over to him. "Hi honey, what's up?"

"I just had a very interesting conversation with one of our new guests. His name is Vandor. He's from the planet Zandrax, and has been living on Earth for the past seventy thousand years."

"Is he mentally stable?"

"Yes, he is. To prove his point, he put his hand on my shoulder and a few seconds later we were in Grand Teton National Park."

"He took you back to Earth in a few seconds? That's incredible! Did he explain how he could do that?"

"He said the people on Zandrax have developed the ability to transport themselves to anyplace they have been before. We're going to continue our conversation tomorrow at two o'clock. I would like you to be there."

"I wouldn't miss it for anything. It's not often you get to talk to a person who has lived through all of Earth's recorded history."

"It's not just the Earth's history I'm interested in. I want to know something about the future, and he said he wanted to discuss that with me."

180

That evening Jeffery and Debbie decided on a list of questions they were going to ask Vandor. It took a few hours because they wanted the questions to be about historically significant events.

Jeffery and Debbie arrived at the restaurant fifteen minutes early. They both ordered coffee. While they were drinking their coffee, Jeffery kept scanning the list of questions.

Vandor arrived at exactly two o'clock. Jeffery looked up at him as he walked up to their table and said, "Good afternoon Vandor. This is my wife Debbie. I hope it's okay for her to join us?"

"Of course, I expected you to bring her." Then he looked at Debbie and said, "It is a pleasure to meet you Debbie. I assume Jeffery told you all about our conversation yesterday."

"Yes, he did, and I am still a little bit skeptical, but Jeffery is convinced you are who and what you claim to be."

"If you need proof we could continue this conversation on Earth? Just tell me where you want to go and I can take us there in a few seconds."

"I don't think that's necessary."

"Okay, did you prepare some questions for me."

Jeffery said, "Yes we did. What can you tell me about the birth of Christianity?"

"Not much. I was appalled by the excesses of the Roman Empire. Their total lack of compassion regarding human life was disgusting. I thought about the possibility of intervening in some of their never-ending wars on the side of their enemies, but I went to China instead. They were also cruel, but not to the same extent as the Romans. The Chinese were, by far, the most advanced civilization on Earth at that time. Anyway, by your calendar I was in China for the hundred years before the birth of Christ and for almost two hundred years after. The Romans were completely intolerant of any people who did not believe in their Gods. By the

181

time I returned to that area the Roman Empire was already showing signs of disintegration. I believe their quest to kill all the Christians was one of the primary factors in their demise."

Jeffery said, "That's a little disappointing. I wasn't expecting you to have been a guest at the "last supper", but I was hoping you would have some firsthand knowledge of Christ's life. I'm not religious but it would have been interesting if you had been able to provide any details of his life. Religion has all but disappeared on Earth, and there has never been any serious religious movement on Procolt 2.

"We have found that as civilizations develop they all go through a phase where religion, or at least the belief in a supreme being, is the driving force that first binds people together. It is an absolute requirement in the formation of all advanced civilizations. People need a logical explanation for birth and death, and religion is an easy way to do that. But as the people's knowledge of science and medicine increases, their need for religion diminishes. Also, as their understanding of the natural world increased, many people became convinced that instead of there being a supreme being, there was a much more advanced civilization that "designed" the plants and animals that lived on their planets."

Debbie responded, "You must admit that living creatures are enormously complex, and the chance that something as complex as a human being could be created entirely by random mutations of less complex lifeforms is extremely unlikely."

"Yes, you're correct. That's why many believe they have been "designed". At the time we began interstellar space travel there was a strong religious belief we had been created by God, and our purpose was to spread humanity throughout the galaxy. For almost a billion years the people of Zandrax played "God" on countless planets, so I suppose we have been the designers of thousands of civilizations. Even though we have created civilizations and populated planets with humanoids for almost a

182

billion years, and we have traveled all over the galaxy, we still have no clue about our own origin. The firm belief in God and religion has almost disappeared among the people on Zandrax too, but there is still a substantial portion of our population that believe we were "designed" by some species more advanced than ours."

Jeffery said, "Let's change the subject a little. One of the things about our history that has bothered me for a long time is how civilizations that were separated by vast distances and had no interaction with other civilizations all utilized pyramids as a religious symbol. Were you responsible for that?"

"Yes, I suppose I was. Pyramids are easy to build and are very durable, so they make ideal religious symbols."

"Many of the primitive societies utilized human sacrifices as part of their religious ceremonies. Are you responsible for that too?" Debbie asked.

"Those sacrifices were part of their ceremonies long before I got involved with them. I did my best to convince them it was wrong and unnecessary to kill people to appease their Gods, but they didn't believe me. They had, what they thought was evidence, the sacrifices were effective. They told me the sacrifices ended droughts and stopped epidemics on numerous occasions. We know it was coincidental, but it was impossible for me to convince them."

"Our ancestors were often very cruel people, but that began to change prior to what we called the 'dark ages'. Did you push us in the right direction?" Jeffery asked.

"That's an interesting question. I was involved with some of the early attempts at democratic reform. As Christianity spread all over Europe it became the center of human development. By the year 1000, Europe was ruled by kings, whose power was absolute. Absolute power is always corrupting, so I put myself in situations where I hoped I could foster the development of more democratic forms of government. My first real attempt was to convince the Archbishop of Canterbury to write the Magna Carta. It was designed to limit the power of the king with respect to the church and the barons, who were in charge of the local populations. It really didn't accomplish very much, but it was the first attempt."

"I also helped the rebels during the French revolution, believing they would establish a democracy if they were successful in overthrowing the king. However, after the rebels won they proved to be as bad, and in some cases much worse, than the king. Nothing really changed until after the United States was formed and became somewhat successful. They established the first real democracy with a government that was elected by the people. It was the first time a country's leaders were not chosen based on family. However, even though the government was elected by the people, it did not prevent them from mistreating many of the people who lived there. It took almost ninety years for them to abolish slavery, and another forty years before they began to treat the people they referred to as 'Indians', with a modicum of respect and dignity."

Jeffery said, "If I remember my history right, the last remnants of prejudice weren't eliminated until about the year 2040."

"You're right, and there was a brief resurgence of prejudice when the first aliens began arriving on Earth, but it ended quickly." Vandor responded.

"Yesterday, you said that you helped Albert Simpson invent the power module. Why did you do that?"

"It was all part of a long term strategy to force Earth to develop interstellar space travel. I worked with Albert's father in propulsion development and when he retired I took over his position. I provided Albert with the original list of elements to be used in the alloys he was testing. I thought it would take him a few years to find the magic combination, but it only took a few weeks.

It was a pleasant surprise. I knew enough about him to know he would immediately realize how to utilize the alloy to make the power module. Almost anyone with a knowledge of physics and electronics would have quickly known that the silver alloy could be used to make an unlimited self-contained source of electrical power."

"I suppose you also had a hand in creating the silver shortage that started us on the road to interstellar space travel?" Debbie asked.

"Not directly. I knew that eventually the Earth would run out of silver, but it also happened much sooner than I expected. I knew about the extensive silver deposits on Ganymede, so I made sure a probe was sent there. The rest was just a happy coincidence. I didn't know a ship from Coplent was going to steal the probe, but it all worked out. I couldn't have planned it better."

"Did you have a hand in Debbie and I being selected for the test of the Star Rover?"

"Absolutely. I had decided, after doing some extensive research on NASA employees, you were the most logical choice. I used my position at NASA to lobby for you. Despite my involvement in the design of the Star Rover, it still contained a lot of untested technology. That made the selection of the captain extremely important. I expected there to be problems and I knew there wasn't anybody more qualified to handle the unexpected than you."

"I also knew about your relationship with Debbie. I know you tried to keep it a secret, but it was actually common knowledge among NASA pilots. I was confident that you would choose her to assist you on the mission, and I thought the two of you could solve any problem that arose."

"That's quite a complement, thank you," Debbie said.

"You're welcome, but the complement was well deserved. I followed your exploits and, although I had never met either of you, I was sure that once you came to Procolt 2 you would fall in love with it and want to stay. When Garlut and Brealak came to Earth for the meeting with the World Council I sent them a report regarding Procolt 2. I'm sure they he had no idea why they received the report. I knew after your first mission you would want to go someplace with a friendlier environment. I was sure you would ask Garlut about it, because there was no one else to ask. I hoped he would remember the report on Procolt 2 and suggest you go there. Obviously, that worked."

"I suppose you knew we would discover the squirrels."

"Yes, I had them put there so they would be mutated into the species they are today. If you hadn't figured out how intelligent they were I was prepared to intervene. I'm really glad that wasn't necessary."

"Did you make us want to build a resort, or was that a coincidence?" Debbie asked.

"I needed you and Jeffery to come here to live so you would be exposed to the radiation. I was certain you would like it here, and I was fairly sure you would figure out something that would allow you to live here. I told Jeffery yesterday that our analysis indicated somebody from Earth would build a resort here. I have friends in high places on Coplent and they were prepared to do whatever was required to make sure the resort was built."

Jeffery said, "Why did you need us to come here, as opposed to some other couple?"

"Although you were the best qualified people for the mission, there was another reason I wanted you on the Star Rover. I wasn't going to tell you this for a while, but I really don't see any reason to wait. Both of you have an uncommon active gene. It makes you more susceptible to the effects of the radiation. The first people from Earth who came here lived to be about one hundred eighty. You two will probably exceed that by two hundred percent, and so will all of your offspring."

186

"So, Jeffery and I are going to live to be more than five hundred years old?" Debbie asked with obvious disbelief in her voice.

"Unless you die as a result of an accident. The combination of the gene and the radiation make you, and your children, virtually immune to disease. I would guess you won't even notice anything you would associate with growing older until you are close to five hundred."

"How common is this gene we both have?" Jeffery asked.

"It occurs once in every twenty-five thousand births. The odds of a couple having the gene is so rare it may have never occurred before. I was prepared to work with any couple where one of them had the gene, but when I found the two of you I knew you would be perfect for the task I am going to ask you to perform."

"What task would that be?" Jeffery asked.

"One I'm not prepared to discuss with you yet, but I will answer any other questions you have."

Jeffery was silent for a few moments and then he asked, "Were you involved in the American Revolution?"

"Not at the beginning. I was in France when the war started, and I met Benjamin Franklin when he assumed his position as ambassador. We had several conversations regarding the American Revolution. I was very impressed with their plans for a democratic government, so I traveled to North America for the first time. I was appalled at the condition of George Washington's army and I wanted to help, but there was very little I could do. I knew how to make weapons that were far more advanced than the muskets they were using, but they didn't have the equipment and raw materials I needed to build them. So, all I could do was watch from the sidelines as they lost most of their battles. I was finally able to help defeat the British at the Battle of the Chesapeake. The French and the British were evenly matched, and the battle was a stalemate. I was aboard one of the French ships and I had a small weapon that could easily sink the British ships without being obvious. I sunk four of them, and that was enough to turn the tide. The French won the battle and the British were unable to bring in reinforcements to assist General Cornwallis in Yorktown. That ultimately resulted in the Americans winning the war."

"Weren't you concerned about getting injured or killed? Medicine at that time was very crude."

"You're right, doctors were, for the most part, useless. But I have an implant in my body that constantly measures my blood pressure, pulse rate, blood chemistry, and brain function. If it detects any anomaly I am instantly transported back to Zandrax where I would receive immediate medical attention. Unless I was killed in a massive explosion I would probably be able to recover."

"So, if you fell down and broke your leg you would disappear?"

"Yes, instantly. However, if it was just a broken bone I'd be back in a about an hour."

"Did you get involved in any of the wars in the twentieth century?"

"No. Shortly after the American Revolution I went back home and didn't return to Earth for about two hundred years. It's probably better I wasn't on Earth for the second world war. I'm not sure I would have allowed either side to develop nuclear weapons. Fission bombs based on uranium or plutonium are extremely inefficient and cause more deaths from radiation exposure than the actual explosion. Fusion bombs based on hydrogen are more efficient, but the radiation is still more deadly than the explosion."

"What types of weapons do you have on Zandrax?"

"We primarily use particle beam weapons, like the type you have on your starships. We have very small ones like this." Then Vandor reached into his pocket and took out a small plastic rectangle and put it on the table in front of Jeffery. Then he said, "That's the weapon I used to sink the British ships."

"How powerful is it? It looks like a toy."

"At its maximum setting, it's probably twice as powerful as the weapons you have on your starship. A starship mounted version would be capable of destroying an entire planet, but we've never done that. I believe that the largest thing we ever destroyed was an asteroid that was about sixty units in diameter. It was going to crash into one of our moons and would have caused catastrophic damage."

"If you were on Earth during the second world war would you have helped the allies win the war?"

"Yes, I've thought about that often. I find it difficult to believe that any sane person could have believed in Hitler's policies. I'm not sure what I would have done, but I would not have allowed Germany and Japan to win the war."

"When did you come back to Earth?"

"I don't remember the exact date, but it was during Bill Clinton's second term as president. When I returned I decided I wanted to work for NASA, so I hacked into the databases of several of the most prestigious universities in the United States and created multiple advanced degrees for myself. I also built a file on myself in the US government databases. It was never necessary before, but by that time people only trusted what they could see on computer generated reports. In any case, it was sufficient for me to get a job as an engineer at the NASA facility in Houston. I was assigned to propulsion system development, and that was where I met Albert Simpson's father, Charles."

"Were you trained as an engineer?"

"Yes, all the children on Zandrax are extensively educated. Our basic education takes twenty-five years. Then, if you want to work as a professional, you may need up to another ten years of education."

189

"You said the radiation on Procolt 2 is similar to the radiation on Zandrax. Do you have the same problems with impotence that we have experienced?"

"Yes, we've found that all the races with long life spans have problems producing offspring. However, the effect of the radiation on impotence diminishes quickly when exposure stops. Since the radiation on Zandrax is natural, we can't limit exposure. As a result, our population is stable, at about five billion people. Each year two million die, and the same number are born. Because there are thousands of schools spread all over the planet, it means the schools don't have a lot of students, so each child receives a lot of personal attention during their education. We all receive education in science, math, engineering, and medicine. That doesn't mean we're all doctors, but we all know a lot more about our bodies than we probably need to."

"Does that mean that if Debbie and I leave Procolt 2 we could have more children?"

"Definitely. It would take a year for the effects to completely dissipate. You'll be pleased to know leaving would have no effect on your increased life span."

"That's interesting," Debbie said. Then she looked at Jeffery and asked, "Do you think Mystic would like a little brother or sister?"

"Mystic is seventy-three; I don't really know how she would feel about a new baby in the family. Anyway, I don't really want to leave Procolt 2. Do you?"

"No, I like our life here."

Vandor said, "Tomorrow let's get together again at the same time. We'll discuss the future. Is that okay?"

Jeffery and Debbie both said, "Yes," at the same time.

They all arrived at the restaurant at the same time the next afternoon. After they were seated Vandor said, "Yesterday I told you I have a task for you. I wanted to go back to Earth and get some information before our meeting, and I did that last night. The task I would like you to do is similar to what you did here on Procolt 2. The genetic engineers on Zandrax believe we may have finally found a way to create the ultimate human species. One that does not have the greed that many of the people on Earth possess or the tendency to have fits of rage like the people on Zandrax. The key to that is the gene both of you have. We have been studying people with that gene for more than a hundred years and found that in addition to making them more susceptible to the effects of the radiation, they have more mellow personalities."

Debbie asked, "So, you want Jeffery and I to populate a whole planet? I don't think we're capable of that, although it might be fun to try."

Vandor smiled and said, "That's not exactly what I had in mind. What I want you to do is select five hundred people from Earth who have the gene to go with you to a new planet and start a new species. I have a list with almost three thousand names on it. The list, in addition to the name, also contains a brief description of the person's education, job history, and any remarkable achievements."

"What do you consider a 'remarkable achievement'?" Jeffery asked.

"One of the people on the list won a Nobel Prize for literature."

"Okay, I agree. That's definitely a remarkable achievement. Tell me about the planet."

"It's at the edge of the galaxy. There are very few solar systems in that region. In fact, the closest neighbor is twelve hundred light years away. The planet is very much like Earth. Unlike Procolt 2, the temperate zone starts eight hundred units north or south of the equator, and extends 1100 units in the direction of the pole. The surface of the planet is covered with several large oceans that cover about sixty-five percent of the surface. The planet is eight percent smaller than Earth, so the gravity is slightly less. The atmosphere is primarily nitrogen and oxygen, although the oxygen level is about ten percent higher than it is on Earth. It has almost no indigenous land animals, and the ones we have seen are all small mammals, nothing much bigger than a rat. Also, all the land animals are herbivores. There are insects and birds, but we have not had an opportunity to study them very much. The oceans are much different; they are filled with life. We've discovered more than a thousand different species of animals in the oceans. By the way, the oceans are fresh water."

"Are there mountains, rivers, and lakes too."

"Yes, the land in the temperate area is covered with dense forests. It's a beautiful and very tranquil place."

"It seems to me we will be very isolated. How will we get the supplies we'll need?"

"We're building a transporter system that will allow people and materials to travel to Zandrax instantly, but we are hoping you will be able use the resources on the planet for your needs. We'll build homes and other infrastructure buildings for the people who move there initially. There will be a small hospital, but you will have to supply the staff. We'll also supply you with the tools you will need to clear land for farming, and build whatever else you need. I'm hoping the transporter would only be used in case of an emergency. We want you to be self-sufficient."

"Can we bring animals from Earth?" Debbie asked.

"I was going to get to that later, but since you asked, I'll tell you about that now. In order to increase the life spans of the initial people who populate, we are going to install radiation sources. But they will be different from the radiation sources we have used previously. Because the people there will have the gene, the radiation will be much weaker than what we have used previously. It will have no effect on animals from Earth, so you can bring whatever you want. Also, it will probably only be needed

192

for five or six years. As you know, while you are exposed to the radiation there are problems with impotence, so if we are trying to build a new species, making them impotent is counterproductive."

Jeffery asked, "Would it be possible to build the transporter to go to Earth instead of Zandrax?"

"Yes, it's possible, but it's not a good idea. We really want you to break your ties with Earth. If we built a transporter that allowed you to go to Earth I'm concerned that you would become dependent on it. Additionally, we don't want additional people from Earth coming to the planet."

"I guess that makes sense. It's just that we're asking the people who come with us to sever all the ties they have with friends and family. That's difficult for a lot of people."

"That's why I'm giving you a list with so many names on it. If there's going to be a problem, select somebody else."

"What if somebody changes their mind after they get there? Can they go back?"

"Only if they can build their own starship. This is a one-way trip. The people are all volunteers and you have to make it clear to them that if they decide to go they will spend their lives on the new planet. That's true for both of you as well."

Jeffery said, "I understand. I think Debbie and I need to discuss this before we make a decision."

Debbie nodded her head in agreement and asked, "I know it's not important, but does this planet have a name?"

"No, you can name it whatever you want."

"Janus is the Roman God of beginnings, so how about if we call it Janus?" Debbie suggested.

"I like it," Jeffery agreed.

"Okay, henceforth we will call it Janus.

"Debbie and I will discuss this and we'll try to have an answer for you by tomorrow afternoon."

"There is no rush. Please take as much time as you need. I want you to be positive that your decision is the right one for both of you. I'll be here again tomorrow afternoon." Then Vandor got up and left.

Jeffery looked at Debbie and said, "Our lives here have become boring. We're simply not needed here. Mystic is running the place without our help. The government is doing a good job. I've been thinking about going back into space and doing some exploring, but this sounds better."

"Our lives may be boring, but they are comfortable. Are you ready to go back to eating food from a replicator?"

"Yes, we've been here for almost a hundred years. I want change. I also think it would be nice to have more children. I think I'm ready to be a father again."

"You know we'll never see Mystic or William again. I'm not sure I'm okay with that."

"I understand, and I'll miss them too. Of course, William is working on Earth now so we only see him once a year. Tomorrow I'll ask Vandor about it. Perhaps he could bring Mystic and William there to visit once in a while."

"Let's not ask, let's make it a condition if we agree to do this. I'll bet all the people on Vandor's list are single. We'll probably be the only people on Janus with a child and a grandchild, so it won't seem as if we are receiving special treatment."

"Are you saying you want to do this?"

"Right now, I'm saying I want to think about it for a while. I know how you feel, and to some degree I feel the same way. I just want to be sure."

Jeffery and Debbie were up most of the night discussing the pros and cons of Vandor's plan. By morning they had made the decision to do it as long as Vandor agreed to bring Mystic and William to Janus occasionally.

Jeffery and Debbie were eating breakfast in the restaurant when Mystic walked up to their table. When she was a few feet away Jeffery said, "Good morning. You look bright and cheerful this morning. What's going on?"

"I'm pregnant. I never thought it would happen again, but it did. I haven't told Virgil yet, but I know he'll be pleased. I'm not sure how William will feel about having a baby brother or sister.

"Congratulations honey, I know how much you wanted another child," Jeffery said happily.

"I'm so happy for you!" Debbie exclaimed.

"I have to go tell Virgil and send a message to William. I'll talk to you later. Bye."

After Mystic walked away Debbie said, "I guess that changes our plans. I'm not going anywhere while Mystic is pregnant."

"I agree, but perhaps Vandor can put everything off for a year. I don't think this was going to happen very quickly anyway."

"Okay, let's discuss this with him this afternoon."

That afternoon Jeffery, Debbie, and Vandor all arrived at the table at the same time again. Vandor said, "I heard Mystic is pregnant. Congratulations. Soon you'll have another grandchild."

"How did you find out?" Debbie asked.

"It's not a secret. I think everybody who works here knows. Pregnancies are not very common on Procolt 2, so they are always news," Vandor responded.

"I was wondering why everyone was smiling at us, now I know. I guess you and I are a little out of touch with the other people here," Jeffery said.

Debbie said, "We were ready to accept your offer, if you agreed to some conditions, and then we found out about the pregnancy. This changes everything."

Vandor smiled and said, "This plan will take at least two years to implement. The baby will be born long before you have to leave to go to Janus."

"If we agree to do this, can you bring Mystic and her family to Janus to visit occasionally?" Jeffery asked.

"I'm sure that could be arranged, but since Mystic has the gene, perhaps she and her family would like to be part of the initial group on Janus. I know her husband doesn't have the gene, but we could make an exception in his case. You must realize that because Mystic has the gene she will probably outlive her husband by more than three hundred years. She would probably be more comfortable with people who have the same life span she does."

"I hadn't thought about that," Debbie said.

"I think we need to have a talk with our daughter about all this."

After the meeting with Vandor, Debbie called Mystic and said, "Something very important has come up and we need to have a family meeting this evening."

"Mom, we haven't had a family meeting since I was a teenager. What's going on?"

"I'd rather discuss the situation with you in person."

"Should I bring Virgil?"

Debbie hesitated for a few seconds and then said, "I don't think that's a good idea. You'll have to discuss the situation with Virgil, but right now I want to make this just between the three of us."

"Okay, I'll be there at eight."

Mystic walked into their apartment a few minutes early. Debbie and Jeffery were sitting in the living room when Mystic arrived. She walked in and asked, "What's the big mystery? Is there something wrong?"

Jeffery said, "Please sit down. Something has happened that you need to be informed about. It concerns the whole family."

Mystic sat down, stared at Jeffery, and said, "Okay Dad, tell me the bad news."

"Three days ago a man arrived here. I was there to meet the ship. He came up to me and told me his name was Vandor and he needed to discuss the past and future with me. He said he was human, but not from Earth. I thought he was some kind of nut and then he put his hand on my shoulder. We were instantly transported back to Earth. I suddenly found myself in Grand Teton National Park. Then a minute later he brought us back."

"Dad, are you sure this wasn't a dream or something?"

"Yes, I'm sure it wasn't a dream. We went into the restaurant and he told me some amazing stuff."

For the next ten minutes Jeffery gave mystic a synopsis of his first conversation with Vandor. When he was finished Mystic said, "So, this person has been controlling the destiny of human life on Earth for all of recorded history. That's hard to believe."

"I understand your skepticism. The next afternoon your mother and I met with him. We asked him questions about Earth's history. We obviously have no way of verifying the things he said, but I believe him. Then he said he wanted to meet with us again to discuss the future, because he was trying recruit your mother and I for a substantial task."

"Did he want money?"

"No, the subject never even came up. Yesterday he told us that your mother and I both have a gene that makes us more susceptible to the effects of the radiation here. In fact, he made sure I was selected to be the pilot of the Star Rover, and he was positive I would choose your mother to be my assistant. Yesterday he told us that people with the gene, and their offspring, would have a substantially longer life. Our lifespans will exceed five hundred years, which means you will outlive Virgil by more than three hundred years. That was why we wanted to meet with you alone."

Mystic was silent for a while, obviously thinking about what her father had just told her. Then she said, "What about William? Does he have the gene?"

"I don't know, but I'm sure we can find out. Every person on Procolt 2 has a complete DNA analysis on file. I don't know what to look for, but I'm positive Vandor does. If William has the gene he needs to know about his increased life span."

"How am I going to tell Virgil about this?"

Debbie said, "I'm not sure you should. What purpose would it serve?"

"None, you're probably right. I shouldn't tell him. For some reason, I'm positive you have more to tell me. What is the task Vandor wants you to do?"

"The people of Zandrax are trying to develop the ultimate human being. They have found a planet at the edge of the galaxy that is very similar to Earth. They want your mother and I, along with five hundred people from Earth who also have the gene, to start a new civilization. If we decide to do it we'll never be back; it's a one-way trip."

Mystic yelled, "You won't be here to watch my new baby, your grandchild, grow up! I don't like that idea at all!"

Debbie said, "Please calm down. First, we haven't told him we would do it yet. Additionally, he promised to bring you and your family there to visit us on a regular basis. He also suggested that you, Virgil, and the new baby could be part of the initial group."

"If I left what would you do with Procolt Paradise?"

"I'd give it to the government. I don't need the money."

"How soon would all this happen?"

"Not less than two years. The plan is to construct a place for us to live and all the necessary infrastructure before we arrive. They're also going to build a transport system between Zandrax and Janus, that's the name of the planet, that can be used in case there's an emergency."

"I have a bunch of questions. Are they going to install radiation sources on Janus? Will there be medical facilities and schools?"

"Vandor said they are going to build a hospital, but we have to staff it. They are going to install radiation sources, but they will be removed after five or six years. That will be sufficient exposure to start the mutation process. I don't think schools will be necessary for about ten years. You know that exposure to the radiation makes people almost impotent. But after the radiation sources are removed fertility returns, and the ability to conceive normally will be restored. If you move there your baby will likely be the only child on Janus for a long time."

"I know you haven't said your definitely going, but I think you're leaning in that direction. Why?"

Jeffery said, "I'm bored. My life is too predictable. I want some adventure in my life again. If we don't do this we're going to take our ship and go exploring for a few years, but this sounds more exciting."

"Can Vandor take us to Janus so we can see it for ourselves?"

"I don't see why not. I'll call him now and ask him."

Jeffery picked his communicator, called Vandor, and explained what he wanted. Vandor said he would be there in a few minutes.

A few minutes later the doorbell beeped. Mystic got up and opened the door for Vandor. He walked in and said, "You must be Mystic. It's a pleasure to meet you. My name is Vandor, but I'll bet you parents already told you that."

"Yes, they did. It's nice to meet you as well. However, I really don't like the fact that you are trying to break up our family."

"I'm not trying to break up your family. I truly believe that your parents are the ideal candidates to manage the development of Janus. I also think you should go with them. You've been running Procolt for almost fifty years, wouldn't it be nice to do something else?"

"You know, I hadn't really thought about that. We have over five thousand employees, and keeping the place running is a lot of work. I haven't even taken a vacation in a couple of years."

"Setting up a new community on Janus will be a lot of work too, but the three of you can share the load. Anyway, your father said that you wanted to see Janus for yourself."

"Yes, but I think all three of us want to go. I'm sure you know I'm pregnant. Is this going to be safe for my baby?"

"Yes, it's perfectly safe," Vandor assured her. Then he walked into the center of the living room and said, "We all must hold hands. I'll take us to the location where we plan to build the town. I don't know the time on Janus; it may be the middle of the night. If that's the case we will do this again in about eight hours."

Debbie and Jeffery stood up and they walked over to Mystic, who was already holding Vandor's hand. They formed a circle and Vandor said, "Here we go!"

At first all they saw was bright white then the view began to change and they were standing in a meadow dotted with tall trees. The sun was either setting or rising, they did not know which.

Mystic looked around. The meadow they were standing in was enormous, and appeared to be surrounded by a dense forest. There were snow-capped mountains off in the distance. Something was bothering Mystic and it took her a few seconds to realize what was wrong. There was no sound. There was a very gentle breeze blowing, but there were no birds or insects. However, the place was beautiful.

"We picked this area because it's near the confluence of three rivers. There are lots of fish in the rivers for food, and the soil

200

is very fertile. It will be easy to grow crops here. And the weather is perfect. In the last three years the lowest temperature was twenty-eight degrees and the highest was seventy-seven."

"That sounds absolutely perfect. What is the annual rainfall?" Debbie inquired.

"It's averaged twenty-four inches per year for the past three years. It does snow occasionally in the winter. The deepest snowfall so far has been six inches, but the snowfalls are usually less than two inches."

"Was this meadow natural, or did you clear the land?" Jeffery asked.

"It was natural. We're about a unit west of the rivers. Do you want to go see them?"

"Yes, I would like that." Mystic responded.

They walked for about a tenth of an hour and the rivers came into view. There were two rivers, each of them more than fifty feet wide, and they connected into a single large river that was at least a hundred feet wide. They walked to the edge of the large river. The water appeared to be moving rapidly. In the water, they could see several different kinds of fish. Some only a few inches long, and others close to three feet in length. The water was crystal clear. It was an idyllic setting.

Jeffery asked, "Why did you decide to build the town a mile from the rivers?"

"Because they occasionally overflow their banks and flood the area nearby. I'm sure we could build something that would prevent the flooding, but we wanted to keep it as natural as possible. The area where we are planning to build is about sixty feet higher, so there's no possibility it would flood."

"What exactly are you planning to build?" Debbie asked.

"Basically, were prepared to build whatever you and Jeffery feel is needed."

"How far are we from Procolt 2?" Mystic asked.

"Five thousand two hundred light years. It will take you about a half a year to get here by ship, and Zandrax will be supplying it. The ship we will be using is much larger than anything you have. Right now, the ship is designed to move only passengers, but it will be modified so that in addition to carrying up to six hundred passengers, it will be able to move hundreds of animals, and any personal items the passengers want to bring with them. Anything else you are likely to need will already be here when you arrive."

Mystic looked around, sighed deeply, and said, "I really like this place. I'd like to bring Virgil here. Can you do that for me?"

"Of course. I really want you to be a part of this. It's obvious you have excellent organizational skills and would be a real asset to the project."

"Thank you. I appreciate that."

"I know this is personal, but I hope you aren't considering telling Virgil about the differences in your life spans. As a matter of fact, I have no intention of telling any of the colonists about it, and I don't want you to either. Because of the advances in medical technology many people on Earth are already living to be more than one hundred thirty, and it's common knowledge that on Procolt 2 life spans are usually more than one hundred eighty. I think we should let them know their life spans will be about the same as they are on Procolt 2. That should be enough to get you all the volunteers you will need."

Jeffery said, "The knowledge regarding the longer lifespans on Procolt 2 has created a problem. We now have a waiting list of more than three million people who want to immigrate there. As a result, we are constantly arresting people who try to go there without first obtaining permission. Many people think it's worth the risk, and if they end up jail for a while it's okay because even in jail they are exposed to the radiation.

However, they are in for a big surprise. We just finished building a facility on Procolt 4 to hold our prisoners and the people currently incarcerated for violation of immigration laws are being moved there. Any new offenders will be sent there awaiting trial, and if found guilty will be sent to the prison there."

"I was not aware of that, but it may resolve the problem. Unless anybody has an objection, I think we should go back now."

Mystic said, "I'm ready to go back home. Can Virgil and I meet with you tomorrow?"

"Yes, I'll meet you by the shuttle pad at ten o'clock."

They all joined hands again and a few seconds later they were standing in Jeffery and Debbie's apartment. After Mystic and Vandor left Debbie asked, "Did you like Janus? I was very impressed."

"Yes, I liked it a lot. It reminded me of what Procolt 2 was like when we first came here. If Mystic likes it too, and I think she does, we should agree to Vandor's plan."

"Yeah, you're right. I think we should probably do it even if Mystic decides not to join us, but I really don't think that will happen."

"Are you going to miss this place? I think I will, at least for a while."

"I suppose I will too, but I'm beginning to like the idea of having some adventure in my life again."

The next morning Vandor took Mystic and Virgil to Janus. Virgil liked it as much as Mystic did, so they made the decision to join the initial group of settlers.

That afternoon Vandor met with Jeffery and Debbie again. He gave them the list of candidates and said, "The selection of people for the group is entirely up to you. Please remember that you will need people with all types of experience to make this a success. You'll need doctors, nurses, carpenters, farmers, plumbers, electricians, and more specialists that I probably haven't thought about. But they all must be willing to do the manual labor required to build your new settlement too."

Jeffery said, "You know Debbie and I have already done that once before, although we didn't have a list of names to choose from. We'll get started on this immediately. We're going to leave for Earth in a few days, and we plan on staying there until we have five hundred candidates selected, and at least fifty alternates."

"That sounds like a good plan. You'll probably be swamped by reporters when you arrive. That would probably be the best way to get the publicity you need so people will know why you are there. That way when you contact prospective candidates they'll have some understanding of your task."

"I'm going to prepare a speech before we leave. When it's finished I'll read it to you and you can make any comments you feel are appropriate."

"Thanks, I'll be happy to do that."

Jeffery and Debbie spent the next day preparing the speech. When it was finished he called Vandor and asked him to come over to critique it. Vandor arrived a half hour later. After he sat down in the living room Jeffery picked up the speech and began to read, "Thank you for this wonderful welcome. Debbie and I are both very happy to be back on Earth again. It has been more than ten years since our last visit. However, we are not here on vacation. We have had a series of meetings with a representative from the planet Zandrax. They are humans, much like us, but their civilization is more than two billion years old. For the last billion years they have been searching the galaxy for planets that would support human life. When they found one they placed radiation sources on the planets and brought primates there, knowing that the radiation would eventually cause the primates to mutate into humanoids. Earth was their most successful test. They are also responsible for the radiation on Procolt 2, although the radiation was put there for a different purpose. Their goal was to create the ultimate human. They knew their own civilization was prone to fits of rage, and they wanted to eliminate that flaw. On Earth they were close, but people from Earth have a major flaw as well. We're greedy, we want what our neighbor has. It doesn't matter if it's power, money, land, water, or anything else. If we want it, some of us will kill to get it."

Jeffery paused for a few moments and then continued to read, "The people from Zandrax look exactly like us, and have been living on Earth, unnoticed, for most the last seventy thousand years. They recently discovered that some of us, including Debbie and I, have a gene which makes us unique. We have no greed, or fits of rage, and the genetic engineers on Zandrax feel that people from Earth with that gene will eventually mutate into what they believe will be the ultimate human. They have found a planet with an environment almost identical to Earth's at the edge of the galaxy which we have named Janus. They want Debbie and I to select five hundred people from Earth who have the gene to go with us to Janus and start a new species. We have a list of five thousand people and we will begin contacting them shortly and give them more details. Thank you."

Jeffery put the paper down the paper with the speech and asked, "Did you think that was okay?"

"Yes, I did. You paused at exactly the right time too. I think it will be effective and probably create some controversy, but that is okay. You want people to think about what you said."

"Good, I'm glad you liked it. Debbie and I are leaving tomorrow morning. How long are you staying here?"

"Probably at least another thirty days. I really like it here. Let me know where you are staying and I will stop by occasionally, since it only takes a few seconds to get there."

"I wish I could do that," Debbie said.

"We decided to stay somewhere that's away from crowds in the big cities, so we're going to stay on the space station until the task is completed.

Vandor stood up and as he walked toward the door said, "Okay, I'll stop by in thirty days or so to see how you're doing. Have a good trip."

Three days later their ship was approaching the space station. The ship was automatically identified by the system at the space station and when they were about one hundred thousand units away Jeffery received a call. A young woman asked, "Sir, am I speaking with Admiral Whitestone?"

"Yes, this is Admiral Whitestone, or at least I was Admiral Whitestone until I retired eighty years ago. Please call me Jeffery."

"Sir, that would be disrespectful."

"I promise I won't be offended. My wife and I are here, and will be staying on the space station for a long time. Please let me know where I can park my ship."

"Sir, uh, I mean Jeffery, please land at Shuttle Bay 3. We will park your ship for you. Welcome back to Earth. The Station Master will be there to meet you."

"Thank you. I appreciate the excellent service."

A half hour later Jeffery parked his ship in Shuttle Bay 3. As soon as the bay was pressurized there was a knock on the hatch. Jeffery opened it and a man in a NASA captain's uniform walked into the ship and said, "Sir, I'm Captain Collins. I would like to welcome you to the station. It's an honor to meet both of you. Are you staying on the station or would you like me to book a shuttle for you?"

"Thank you, Captain Collins. We have an open reservation at the Hilton. We will be staying on the station until our task is finished, and that could take ninety days or more.

"Okay, sir."

"Captain Collins, please call me Jeffery, and my wife Debbie. We have been out of NASA for a long time, and even on the ships I commanded everyone called me Jeffery."

"Okay Jeffery, I'm sure you realize you're a legend around here. You probably know that every large city on Earth has a Whitestone High School."

"Yes, I'm aware of that."

"There are two reporters out there waiting to speak to you. I could make them go away if you want me to."

"Instead of making them go away, tell them I will be holding a brief news conference tomorrow morning at ten o'clock. At that time I will make an announcement and answer questions."

"I'll take care of it, Jeffery."

Captain Collins walked out of the bay and came back almost immediately. He said, "They both ran to call their supervisors. I expect you'll have a lot of people at your news conference tomorrow morning."

"Captain, that's exactly what I want."

"Please follow me to the hotel. Leave your luggage. They will send somebody to pick it up."

Jeffery and Debbie walked with Captain Collins to the hotel. When they arrived at the check-in desk the clerk said, "Admiral and Captain Whitestone, it's an honor to meet you. Welcome back! When I saw your reservation, I thought it was someone's idea of a joke, but then I heard your ship was arriving. May I escort you to your room?"

Debbie replied, "Yes, of course."

As they were walking to their room Debbie said, "I remember the first time we stayed here. Garlut and Brealak were in the room next to ours. It's hard to believe that was probably eighty-five years ago."

Jeffery smiled and said, "Yeah, it only seems like fifty."

Debbie said, "You really haven't grown up much in those eighty-five years. You're still a smart ass."

"I know, I guess some things will never change."

The desk clerk opened the door for them and handed each of them a key. Jeffery reached into his pocket, took out a coin, and handed it to the clerk.

"Sir, I appreciate this but I can't take your money. We're not allowed to accept tips anymore."

"Why?"

"First, no one carries cash anymore. We did away with cash about ten years ago. Also, all the employees were given raises to compensate for the loss of tips."

"It's been ten years since our last visit to Earth. Obviously there have been some changes. Anyway, thank you for the service."

"You're welcome."

After the clerk left Debbie said, "This place really brings back memories. It doesn't seem like it's been that long since the first time we came here. I do miss Garlut and Brealak."

"I do too. I think we should go the restaurant and order the same meal we did that first night we were here. I think we ordered lobster bisque, veal cordon bleu, French fries, and creamed spinach."

"That sounds good me. Let's do it."

The next morning Jeffery and Debbie were eating breakfast in the hotel restaurant when a man walked up to their table and said, "I'm sorry to disturb you, but there are at least twenty reporters in the lobby waiting for you to make an announcement. I'm moving them to the large conference room to wait for you. Don't hurry, you said you would speak to them at ten o'clock, so you have a lot of time to finish your breakfast. I'll let them know you will be there at ten."

"Thank you. Where is the conference room?"

"Walk past the front desk and turn left at the hallway. The conference room is the third door on the right. The door has a big 'A' on it."

Jeffery and Debbie walked into the conference room a few minutes before ten. There were probably forty people waiting for him. As he walked in they all stood up and began applauding. Jeffery walked up to the podium, smiled at the audience, and asked them to be seated. He took his prepared speech out of his pocket and read it. When he was finished the room was silent for several seconds. Then the questions started.

"Do you know how the list of names was compiled?"

"No, all I know for sure is that all of the people on the list have the gene."

"Where is Janus?"

"As I said, Janus is at the edge of the galaxy. It's more than five thousand light years from Earth. However, I do not know its exact location."

"Will the people going with you to Janus have extended life spans?"

"Yes, everyone there will be exposed to radiation for five or six years. That exposure will begin the mutation process. The immediate effects of exposure are an increased life span and decreased fertility. Once the radiation sources are removed fertility will return to normal, the extended lifespan is permanent, and will be passed down to all their children."

"Are you taking anything else with you to start your settlement?"

"Yes, we will be taking farm animals, although I am not sure how many at this point. We will also be taking anything our farmers think they will need to grow our food supplies."

"Won't you be using food replicators?"

"Yes, but not for any longer than absolutely necessary. Food replicators are wonderful, but the food is missing some of the more subtle flavors you get with real foods. Try comparing a steak from a food replicator and the real thing. Believe me, there's an obvious difference.

"Have you been to Janus?"

"Yes, both Debbie and I spent an afternoon exploring the area where the settlement will be built. It's a beautiful area and the weather is perfect. The highest temperature during the year is seventy-seven and the lowest is twenty-eight. The area averages about twenty-four inches of rain per year, and does have minor amounts of snowfall in the winter."

"How are you going to get there?"

"Zandrax will be sending a ship to Earth to pick up the people and animals that will make up the settlement."

"Are you concerned about being isolated from the rest of the trade group planets?"

"Yes, I am. The nearest system to Janus is more than a hundred light years away. We will be on our own. Also, because Janus is so remote, this will be a one-way trip. The people who agree to go will be leaving Earth forever."

"If Janus is so remote, how did you get there for an afternoon?"

"I was waiting for somebody to ask that question. The people from Zandrax have the ability to transport themselves instantly to anyplace they have been to before. Additionally, anyone they are in physical contact with is transported as well. They expect humans from Earth will develop that ability as well in the future."

"If we are the end result of an experiment with primates, then I would have to conclude that God was not involved with human development. Do you agree?"

"No, I don't agree. The people from Zandrax believe they have been doing the work God intended for them. We already

210

knew humans were the product of evolution. The only difference is that now we know details we didn't know before."

A few seconds went by and nobody asked a question so Jeffery said, "Thank you all for coming today. I appreciate your help in getting the word out about Janus." Then he took Debbie's hand and left the room.

When Jeffery and Debbie got back to their room Jeffery said, "Before we start contacting people on the list we need to call William. We have to let him know what's going on. I'm sure he saw the news conference."

"I'll call him and explain the situation. If he has the gene he should come. If not, he should probably stay on Earth."

"We should probably check the list to see if William is on it. If he isn't, we'll have to ask Vandor about it."

Debbie turned on her computer and brought up the list. Then she checked to see if William was on it. She yelled, "Great news! William Griffith is on the list! I'm going to call him right now."

William answered the call and Debbie said, "Hi William. It's your Grandmother. How are you?"

"I'm fine. I saw the news conference and I was really surprised. I got a message from Mom telling me she was pregnant again but she didn't mention anything about you and Grandpa coming to Earth."

"William, we're staying on the space station. We haven't seen you for a year. Can you come up here and spend a few days with us? We want to discuss this in person with you."

"Okay, I'll take a shuttle up there tomorrow."

"Perfect, we'll see you then."

Debbie ended the call and said, "William will be here tomorrow. I hope he agrees to go to Janus with us."

"Well, it's our job to convince him. Anyway, now the real task begins. I think we should split this up. One of us should look

211

for doctors and other medical personnel, and the other should look for farmers. Once we have those selected we can work together on finding the other tradespeople we will need."

"Okay, I'll look for the medical people and you can look for farmers."

"Let's get started."

They spent the rest of the day preparing for the calls they would make tomorrow. The entire news conference was broadcast all over the Earth. Jeffery was certain that anyone they called would know about Janus.

By the following morning they were ready to get started. Debbie had a list of twenty-two doctors and thirty-one nurses. It was midday in the North American Union so she made the first call there. She called the first doctor on her list, Michael Frost.

A woman answered the phone, "Dr. Frost's office. How can I help you?"

"My name Debbie Whitestone. Would it be possible to speak to Dr. Frost?"

"Oh my God! Are you the famous Debbie Whitestone?"

"I suppose so."

"Wow! Please hold for a moment."

About a minute later a man said, "This is Dr. Frost. How can I help you?"

"Dr. Frost, this is Debbie Whitestone. Did you see my husband's news conference yesterday?"

"It would have been hard to miss it since it was repeated so many times."

"You are the first person we are calling regarding the Janus mission. Would you be interested in joining us?"

"You know, since I saw that new conference yesterday I have been thinking about what I would say if I was asked that question. I must say I never really expected it to happen, but now that it has, I'm not sure. I like the adventure and the idea of starting a new civilization, but Earth is all I know. I've never even been to the space station."

"Dr. Frost, we will be somewhat isolated, so we need the best medical personnel we can find. Your references are excellent and I'm sure you would be a real asset to the group. Zandrax is building a hospital for us, so we will have the most modern equipment available. Probably even things that aren't available on Earth yet."

"Would I be able to pick my staff?"

"If they're on the list that wouldn't be a problem. If they aren't on the list then we would have to verify they have the gene before we could accept them."

"What do you know about the gene?"

"Nothing, other than it's relatively rare. It occurs once in every twenty-five thousand births."

"Everyone on Earth has a complete DNA analysis on file. Can you find out what gene we are looking for?"

"Yes, I'm sure I can do that. I'll call you back as soon as I can."

After she ended the call she said, "I wasn't expecting that. We need more information about the gene."

"I'll send a message to Vandor and ask him to come here."

"That's a good idea."

They were discussing their plans for the day when there was a knock on the door. Jeffery answered it and was surprised and pleased to see William standing there.

William had a big smile on his face and said, "Hi Grandpa." Then William and Jeffery hugged briefly and William walked in. He went over to Debbie, kissed her on the cheek and said, "Hi Grandma. It's really nice to see both of you."

Debbie said, "It's wonderful to see you too. I hope you didn't have a problem getting time off to come here."

"Didn't Mom tell you I bought the company last year? Since I own it getting time off is not a problem."

"No, she never mentioned that. That must have happened after your last visit to Procolt 2."

"Yeah, right after. Mom gave me the money to buy it while I was there."

Jeffery said, "That may complicate things a bit. Please sit down William, we have something very important to discuss with you."

William sat down on one of the recliners and said, "Okay, let's talk."

Jeffery said, "Your name is on the list of potential Janus settlers. Your Mother, Father, and their new baby will be coming with us. We want you to go there too."

"I like my life here and I really don't want to go live in a primitive settlement."

"There are some things you don't know. You grew up on Procolt 2 and were exposed to the radiation there during that whole period of your life. That means you already have an increased life span. What you don't realize is that because you have the gene you will live to be well over the age of five hundred."

"I have a girlfriend now, and we have talked about getting married. I don't want to leave her."

"I understand, but you should know that you will outlive her by hundreds of years. She will begin to show her age while you will still look and feel like a young man."

William was silent for a while, then he asked, "What if Tina has the gene too?"

"Even if Tina has the gene she has to be exposed to the radiation for five or six years to be affected by it. If she has the gene we can arrange for her to go to Janus as well."

"How can we find out?"

Debbie said, "Give me her last name and I'll check the list. But the list only has three thousand names on it, and there are probably millions of people on Earth with the gene."

"Her last name is Gardner."

Debbie checked the list and her name was not on it. She said, "There is no Tina Gardner on the list. We'll send a message to Vandor and ask him about her."

William was obviously upset by the situation. He said softly, "I don't want to watch her grow old and die by herself. I always thought that was something we would do together."

Jeffery said, "I'm sorry William, but this is something you had to know about."

William said, "I guess all I can do is hope she's has the gene. Please excuse me, I'm going to get a room and think about this for a while. I'll come by later." Then he got up and left.

Debbie said, "That went rather badly."

"I think he just needs some time to work things out. In the meantime, I'll send another message to Vandor and find out if Tina has the gene."

They spent the rest of the day contacting people on the list. Jeffery had much better luck with farmers. He managed to get four who would grow crops and two who would raise cattle and pigs. Every one of them liked the idea of being in new place with new equipment in an area that had a "small town" environment.

Debbie only enlisted one doctor. Dr. Thomas Jarvis was a surgical resident at a large hospital near New York City, and like the farmers, he longed to live in a small town. He really wanted to have the freedom to spend whatever time he felt was appropriate with his patients, not the time dictated by the insurance companies. He also offered to help Debbie with her enlistment of other medical personnel, which she gratefully accepted. Dr. Jarvis asked Debbie to send him the list of other potential candidates with medical backgrounds, which she sent out immediately.

215

That evening Jeffery and Debbie decided they would need, at the most, four doctors, six nurses, and ten farmers. In Jeffery's conversations with the farmers he told them they would each have two hundred fifty acres. Every one of the crop framers said they didn't need that much land to grow food for only five hundred people. The two livestock farmers felt that much land would be very helpful. Jeffery also told them that all the farmers would get together and discuss what to grow and how much to plant before they left for Janus. That way they would be able to bring any supplies they would need on the trip.

The following day the recruiting went much better. With Dr. Jarvis's help Debbie was able to recruit three more doctors, including Michael Frost. They also managed to find three nurses. Jeffery also signed up the rest of the farmers they would need.

When they were done for the day Jeffery said, "Every person I spoke to had already been thinking about Janus before we called them. I'm sure the news conference was responsible for that."

"I'm sure your correct. The cities on Earth are magnificent places, but they are all overcrowded. Moving to Janus allows people to live a more relaxed lifestyle and I think that was a factor as well."

"Nobody mentioned living longer, but I'll bet they were all thinking about it."

"Yeah, I was actually surprised nobody asked about it."

"So, tomorrow you need to find three more nurses. I'll start on the tradespeople we will need.

The following morning they went to a restaurant for breakfast. They were discussing their tasks for the day when they realized someone was standing next to their table. Jeffery looked up and was surprised to see Vandor.

Vandor smiled at him and said, "I received your message."

"Thanks for coming, please join us."

Vandor sat down and said, "Thank you. How are things going?"

"Better than I expected. The medical professionals are no longer questioning ways of identifying the gene. We have four doctors and three nurses. As far as medical personnel are concerned we only need three more nurses. I also signed up ten farmers. I don't think we will need anymore. However, we have a personal issue that I think you can help us with."

"You know I'll help you if I can. What's the problem?"

"Our Grandson, William, is on your list. We spoke to him yesterday and he told us he has a girlfriend named Tina Gardner and he doesn't want to leave her. We need to know if she has the gene."

"I can find the answer to that in just a few moments." Then Vandor sat down at the table and took a small device out his pocket. He gave the device a verbal command that included Tina's name. The device beeped. Vandor looked at the device and the expression on his face changed. He said, "I'm sorry to tell you Tina does not have the gene."

Debbie said, "That's not the answer I was hoping for. I'm not sure what he will do now."

"We're making an exception for Virgil and possibly for Mystic's new baby already. I suppose we could make an exception for Tina as well."

"Jeffery and I will discuss that with him this afternoon."

"Okay, please let me know what he decides. If he would like to visit Janus I'll be happy to take him there. Regarding your selection of medical personnel; I think that's a good start. I probably should have mentioned this before, but we have androids that can assist with most manual tasks. They look and act almost human, they breathe, their eyes blink, and their skin feels human. You can use them to do the chores most people hate, like cleaning.

217

They can also assist the nurses at the hospital or teach when that becomes a requirement."

"I like the idea of using robots to clean, but I think people would appreciate a human taking care of them if they are confined to a hospital. I'll have to think about using androids as teachers, although we already utilize computers extensively in our schools on Procolt 2. I'm not sure there's much difference between the two."

Debbie said, "I realized this morning there was one medical position we forgot about. We're going to have hundreds of farm animals on Janus and I'm sure there will be pets too. We'll need at least two veterinarians. Vandor, are there any on your list?"

"Yes, although I don't remember how many. However, I'm sure there are more than two. Also, regarding the gene, I'm not divulging any information about it at this time. We have searched the DNA scans of almost every human living on Earth, and we know who has the gene. I'm concerned that if more information about the gene was made public people would try to fake having it in order to get on the Janus list."

"Why would we need the list again?" Jeffery asked.

"We have to consider the possibility that many of the original settlers could die from accidents or some unknown disease. If that happened we would need to find replacements."

"We're already picking fifty alternates."

"Yes, but many of them will probably be used to replace any original settlers who change their mind about going. I guarantee you that will happen."

"I think after we select people we should send them to Procolt 2 and have them live there until we are ready to go to Janus. There would be less temptation to change your mind if your away from Earth," Debbie suggested.

Jeffery agreed, "That's a good idea. I'm sure we can find room for them at Procolt Paradise."

Vandor went back to Procolt Paradise to discuss finding space for the Janus settlers with Mystic. Once that situation was resolved he went back to Earth so he could help Jeffery and Debbie.

Later that afternoon William came back to Jeffery and Debbie's room. He did not look happy. He sat down and asked, "Does Tina have the gene?"

Debbie answered, "No, she doesn't. However, Vandor has offered to make an exception so she can go to Janus. Your father is going, and he doesn't have the gene either."

"That's the answer I was expecting. I've decided that in the event Tina didn't have the gene I'm going to stay on Earth so I can be with her."

"I'm not sure you are making the right choice, but if that's what you want to do I will support you. I'm positive your mother won't like your decision either."

"Tina and I love each other, and I want to spend my life with her. Nothing anybody says will make me change my mind."

"Okay, but please try to spend some time on Procolt 2 over the next two years, and bring Tina with you so we can meet her."

"I promise I'll do that, and if Vandor can bring us to Janus occasionally, I will visit there when I can."

"Please send your mother a message today."

"Yes, Grandma. I'm going back to Earth on the next shuttle. I'll send her a message as soon as I get home." Then William walked over to Debbie and kissed her on the cheek again, then he shook Jeffery's hand, and left."

With Vandor's help the entire group of five hundred settlers and fifty alternates were chosen in less than ninety days. During that time, a new facility was completed at Procolt Paradise to house the settlers. Jeffery, Debbie, and Vandor realized that the city Zandrax was building on Janus needed a name, so they decided to call it Janus Prime. The construction of Janus Prime had begun as soon as Jeffery and Debbie agreed to become part of the Janus group, and many of the buildings were completed by the time the last of the settlers were selected.

The Janus settlers were scheduled to arrive at Procolt Paradise in groups of twenty-five every ten days until all five hundred were there. After they were settled into their temporary homes Vandor brought them over to Janus for a brief visit in groups of three or four. Almost all of the settlers were impressed and anxious to get there, but nine of them decided to leave the group. Jeffery selected nine replacements from the group of alternates, so now the group was complete.

Seven months after Jeffery and Debbie returned to Procolt 2, Mystic gave birth to her second child. It was a boy, and Virgil and Mystic named him Toby. A few days after Toby was born a DNA scan was performed. Toby had the gene.

The schedule was set for them to leave Procolt 2 in one hundred twenty days. The ship from Zandrax would make a brief stop at Procolt 2 to pick up the livestock farmers and then go to Earth to pick up the farm animals destined for the farms on Janus. Then it would return to Procolt 2 to pick up the rest of the settlers. The trip to Janus would take one hundred ninety days.

Several of the settlers asked Jeffery why they needed to take a ship to Janus instead of being brought there by Vandor. Jeffery told them the trip would give them the opportunity to get to know each other better and also give them time to delegate tasks for each settler that they would be required to perform once they were living on Janus.

Jeffery and Debbie turned over the ownership of Procolt Paradise and all of their other businesses, with the exception of the research lab, to the government of Procolt 2. They gave the research lab to the squirrels. In order to be sure the squirrels would be able to continue to develop new products, Jeffery and Debbie set up a fund with five million hirodim in it that the squirrels could draw from to fund future projects.

The day before the settlers were scheduled to leave, the staff at Procolt Paradise had a big going away party for Jeffery, Debbie, Mystic, Virgil, and Toby. There were more than a thousand people and several hundred squirrels in attendance. It was a tearful goodbye. The next morning all of the settlers were shuttled to the ship that would take them on the one-way journey to Janus. It was both an end, and a new beginning.

Epilog

The year after the settlers departed from Procolt 2 for Janus, the radiation on Procolt 2 disappeared. It was assumed that people from Zandrax removed the radiation sources, but no one knows for sure. When it became known that the radiation on the planet was gone, the immigration problem disappeared.

For the next two hundred years Earth received only sporadic reports concerning the settlement on Janus. That information was provided by occasional visitors from Zandrax. Despite repeated attempts to find out the location of Janus, our Zandrax visitors refused to divulge the information. They said the civilization on Janus must develop without any outside influence.

There were some brief discussions about attempting to search for the planet, but searching for something more than five thousand light years away is an impossible task. The reports we did receive indicated that everything was going well. Jeffery and Debbie had another child. This time it was a boy, and they named him Zack. Debbie was now the oldest person from Earth to have a child. At the time of Zack's birth, she was one hundred seventy-four years old.

The last report we received from Zandrax concerning Janus was more than a thousand years ago, in 2497. The population on Janus at that time was almost twenty thousand. They were no longer totally dependent on Zandrax for supplies, and as a result no further visits to Janus were planned. However, Zandrax still could be contacted in case of an emergency.

Some other things happened in 2497 too. Zandrax joined the trade group that year and set up transporter stations on Earth and several other trade group planets. The non-human population on Earth exceeded ten percent for the first time and English became the primary language on all trade group planets.

Many of us still wonder about Janus. Only a few years ago, in 3486, a member of the World Council asked a Zandrax trade representative about the possibility of allowing some visitors from Earth to visit Janus using the transporter to first travel to Zandrax and then to Janus. He said he would bring the request to the attention of the Zandrax Leader, but he was sure they would not allow that to happen. So, for the time being, Janus remains a mystery, and is likely to stay that way for many centuries to come.

Made in the
USA
Lexington, KY